Praise for Jonathan Lethem

"A strikingly original collection . . . imaginative, insightful, witty and sad." —*Milwaukee Journal Sentinel*

"An already dazzling writer shows us a new card. . . . *Men and Cartoons* ends on a note that portends Lethem's most experimental turn yet: toward human love as [a transporting] alternate universe. . . . Lethem in a new, more nakedly personal key." —*San Francisco Chronicle*

"Lethem is the man to beat in fiction these days. . . . Every tale of ennui, cosmic regret and petty yearning is perfectly realized. The brevity of the book and perfection of the stories puts every other member of his generation to shame." —*Pittsburgh Post-Gazette*

"Ineffably poignant." —*Time*

"His sheer inventiveness is a treat. . . . Affecting and clever, these tales are standouts." —*People*

"Terrific. . . . Lethem captures the world we know and the one hovering just beyond our periphery." —*The Baltimore Sun*

"A pleasure. . . . These stories offer potent little distillations of Lethem's considerable imagination." —*Entertainment Weekly*

"Compelling. . . . Effective. . . . Intelligent and poignant. . . . Strange, amusing, haunting. . . . Lethem has what musicians call 'chops,' or technical mastery. He can mix and match prose styles and literary genres to create glittering fictional artifacts. . . . Each of these tales rewards the reader in some way—through an insight, a scene or simply the force of the author's imagination." —*St. Petersburg Times*

Jonathan Lethem

Men and Cartoons

Jonathan Lethem is the author of six novels, including *Motherless Brooklyn*, which won the National Book Critics Award, and *The Fortress of Solitude*. He is the author of two short story collections and the editor of *The Vintage Book of Amnesia*. His stories and essays have appeared in *The New Yorker*, *Rolling Stone*, *Granta*, and *Harper's*. He lives in Brooklyn, New York, and in Maine.

Books by Jonathan Lethem

Amnesia Moon

As She Climbed Across the Table

The Disappointment Artist

Girl in Landscape

Gun, with Occasional Music

The Fortress of Solitude

Men and Cartoons

Motherless Brooklyn

This Shape We're In

The Wall of the Sky, the Wall of the Eye

Men and Cartoons

Stories

Jonathan Lethem

VINTAGE CONTEMPORARIES

VINTAGE BOOKS

A DIVISION OF RANDOM HOUSE, INC.

NEW YORK

For Thomas Berger

Versions of some of these stories first appeared elsewhere. "The Vision" (the opening paragraph of which share several sentences with *The Fortress of Solitude,* a novel) was published in *Tin House* and reprinted in *Bestial Noise: The Tin House Fiction Reader.* "Access Fantasy" first appeared in *Starlight 2* and was reprinted in *Histories of the Future.* "The Spray" was published in *Fetish.* "Planet Big Zero" was published in *Lit* and reprinted in *The KGB Bar Reader.* "The Glasses" was published in the *Voice Literary Supplement.* "The Dystopianist, Thinking of His Rival, Is Interrupted by a Knock on the Door" was published in *Conjunctions* and reprinted in *Pushcart Prize Stories XXVIII.* "Super Goat Man" was published in *The New Yorker.* "The National Anthem" was published in *Black Clock* and was reprinted in *Lit Riffs.* "This Shape We're In" was originally published in book form by McSweeney's Books in 2001. "Interview with the Crab" originally appeared in *Bread.*

The Library of Congress has cataloged the Doubleday edition as follows:
Lethem, Jonathan.
Men and cartoons : stories / Jonathan Lethem.—1st ed.
p. cm.
Contents: The vision—Access fantasy—The spray—Vivian Relf—Planet big zero—The glasses—The dystopianist, thinking of his rival, is interrupted by a knock on the door—Super goat man—The national anthem—Interview with the Crab—This Shape We're In.   I. Title.
PS3562.E8544M46 2004   813'.54—dc22   2004050039

Vintage ISBN-10: 1-4000-7680-3
Vintage ISBN-13: 978-1-4000-7680-2

Book design by Lovedog Studio

www.vintagebooks.com

Printed in the United States of America
10 9 8 7 6 5 4 3 2 1

Contents

The Vision   *1*

Access Fantasy   *23*

The Spray   *47*

Vivian Relf   *57*

Planet Big Zero   *75*

The Glasses   *91*

The Dystopianist,
Thinking of His Rival,
Is Interrupted by a
Knock on the Door   *105*

Super Goat Man   *119*

The National Anthem   *149*

This Shape We're In   *161*

Interview with the Crab   *209*

Men and Cartoons

The Vision

I FIRST MET THE KID KNOWN AS THE VISION at second base, during a kickball game in the P.S. 29 gymnasium, fifth grade. That's what passed for physical education in 1974: a giant rubbery ball, faded red and pebbled like a bath mat, more bowled than pitched in the direction of home plate. A better kick got the ball aloft, and a fly was nearly uncatchable—after the outfielder stepped aside, as he or she invariably did, nearly anything in the air was a home run. Everyone fell down, there'd be a kid on his ass at each base as you went past. Alternately, a mistimed kick scudded back idiotically to the pitcher, and you were thrown out at first.

The Vision booted a double. His real name was Adam Cressner, but he believed himself or anyway claimed to be the Vision: the brooding, superpowered android from Marvel Comics' *Avengers*. The comic-book Vision had the power to vary the density of his body, becoming a ghost if he wished to float through walls or doors, becoming diamond hard if he wished to stop bullets like Superman. Adam Cressner couldn't do any of this. This day he wasn't even wearing his cape or costume, but under black curls his broad face was smeared unevenly with red food dye, as it always was. I was fascinated. The Vision had come to be taken for granted at Public School 29, but I'd never seen him up close.

"Nice kick," I ventured, to Adam Cressner's back. The Vision had assumed a stance of readiness, one foot on the painted base, hands dangling between his knees Lou Brock–style. "Ultron-5 constructed me well," replied the Vision in the mournful monotone of a synthetic humanoid. Before I could speak again the ball was in the air, and Adam Cressner had scooted home to score, not pausing as he rounded third.

Now the Vision was a grown man in a sweatshirt moving an open Martini & Rossi carton-load of compact discs into the basement entrance of the next-door brownstone. I spotted Captain Beefheart, Sonny Sharrock, Eugene Chadbourne. I'd been returning from the corner bodega with a quart of milk when I recognized him instantly, even without his red face and green hood, or the yellow cape he'd worn in winter months. "Adam Cressner?" I asked. I made it a question to be polite: it was Adam Cressner.

"Do I know you?" Cressner's hair was still curly and loose, his eyes still wild blue.

"Not really. We went to school together."

"Purchase?"

"P.S. 29, fifth grade." I pointed thumbwise in the direction of Henry Street. I didn't want to say: *You were the Vision, man!* But I supposed in a way I'd just said it. "Joel Porush."

"Possibly I remember you." He said this with a weird premeditated hardness, as if not *remembering* but *possibly remembering* was a firm policy.

"Migrated back to the old neighborhood?"

Cressner placed the box at the slate lip of the basement stairwell and stepped around his gate to take my hand. "By the time we had a down payment we could barely afford this part of the city," he said. "But Roberta doesn't care that I grew up around here. She became entranced with the neighborhood reports in the City section."

"Wife?"

"Paramour."

"Ah." This left me with nothing to say except, "I should have you guys over for drinks."

The Vision lifted one Nimoy-esque eyebrow.

"When you get in and catch your breath, of course." *You and the paramour.*

I met Roberta at the border of our two backyards, the next Sunday. The rear gardens through the middle of the block were divided by rows of potted plants but no fence, allowing easy passage of cats and conversation. These communal yards were a legacy from the seventies that most new owners hadn't chosen to reverse. I had a basement renter's usual garden privileges, and was watering the plants which formed the border when Roberta Jar appeared at her back door. She introduced herself, and explained that she and Cressner had bought the house.

"Yes, I met Adam a few days ago," I said. "I know him, actually. From around here."

"Oh?"

I'd supposed he'd told of our encounter in front, mentioned being recognized by a schoolmate. Now I had to wonder whether to explain Cressner's childhood fame. "We were at grade school together, on Henry Street. Long before this was a fashionable address. Surely he's walked you past his alma mater."

"Adam doesn't reminisce," said Roberta Jar coolly and, I thought, strangely. The assertion which could have been fond or defiant had managed to be neither. I thought of how Adam had *possibly remembered*, the week before.

"Funny, I do nothing else," I said. I hoped it was a charming line. Roberta Jar didn't smile, but her eyes flashed a little encouragement.

"Does it pay well?" she asked.

"Only when something gets optioned for the movies."

"How often is that?"

"It's like the lottery," I said. "Ninety-nine percent of the time, nothing. But that one time and you're golden."

I'd been blunted from the fact of my instinctive attraction to Roberta Jar, in those first moments, by her towering height. Roberta was six two, or three, I calculated, and with none of that hunched manner with which women apologize for great height or sizable breasts. So I'd been awed before being struck. By this time, though, I was struck too. *Paramour-pyramid-pylon*, I fooled with in my head.

I mentioned again having the two of them over for a drink. My evenings were very free since parting from Gia Maucelli, and I was stuck on what I'd blurted to Adam Cressner and had visualized ever since—a grown-up encounter, involving wine and sophisticated talk. No longer a couple, I still socialized like one in my imagination. Cressner and his tall woman would visit my apartment for drinks. They'd see the couple I'd been by Gia's phantom-limb absence, and ratify the couple I'd likely be again by the fact of themselves. In other words, perhaps Roberta Jar had a friend she could set me up with.

"Maybe," she said, utterly disinterested. "Or you could come along tonight. We're having a few people in."

"A housewarming party?"

"Actually, we're playing a game. You'd like it."

"Truth-or-dare, spin-the-bottle sort of thing?"

"More interesting than that. It's called Mafia. You should come—I think we still need a fifteenth."

For bridge or a dinner party you might need a fourth or a sixth—Roberta Jar and Adam Cressner needed a fifteenth. That was how close to essential I'd been encouraged to feel myself to be.

"How do you play Mafia?"

"It's hard to explain, but not to play."

I turned up with wine, still imposing my paradigm, but it was a beer thing I'd turned up at. Adam Cressner ushered me into the parlor, which was restored—new white marble fireplace and mantel, freshly remodeled plaster-rosette ceiling, blond polished floor—but unfurnished, and full instead of gray metal folding chairs like those you'd find in a church basement. The chairs were packed with Adam and Roberta's friends, all drinking from bottles and laughing noisily, too caught up to bother with introductions—when I counted I found myself precisely fifteenth. Roberta Jar was part of the circle, tall in her chair. I wondered if she stood taller than Adam—this was the first time I'd seen them together.

Adam had just been explaining the game, and he started again for me. I was one of four or five in the group who'd never played. Others threw in comments and suggestions as Adam explained the rules. "I'll be the narrator," Adam told us. "That means I'm not playing the game, but leading you through it."

"We want you to play, Adam," someone shouted. "Someone else can narrate. We've played, we know how."

"No, you need a strong narrator," said Adam. "You're an unruly bunch." I imagined I heard in his tone a hint of the Vision's selfless patronage of humanity.

According to the rules of Mafia, the group of fourteen comprised a "village"—except that three of us were "mafia" instead: false villagers working to bring the village down. These identities were assigned by dealt cards, black for village, red for mafia. The game then unfolded in cycles of "night" and "day." Night was when we closed our eyes and lowered our heads—"The village is asleep," Adam explained—with the exception of the three mafiosi. They instead kept their eyes open, and by an exchange of glances silently conspired to select a villager to kill. The victim would be informed of his or her death by the narrator, when night was over, and then make an orderly exit from the game.

Day, by contrast, was chaos, a period of free talk and paranoia among the sincere and baffled villagers—who, of course, included three dissembling mafiosi. Each day closed with the village agreeing by democratic vote on a suspect to banish. This McCarthyesque ritual lynching brought about night, and another attack from the mafia. And so on. The mafia won if they winnowed the village down to two or three, a number they could dominate in any voting, before the village purged all mafiosi from its ranks. It seemed to me like relentless jargonish nonsense, but I worked on a beer (telling Roberta the wine was "for the cellar"), checked out the women, and allowed myself to be swept into the group's flow. We began our first day in the village, peppered by Adam-the-narrator's portentous reminders, such as "Dead, keep your silence." I'd drawn a black card: villager.

Our village was young and boisterous, full of hot, beer-bright faces whose attachments I couldn't judge. It was also splendidly bloodthirsty. "It pretty much doesn't matter who we vote out on the first day," some veteran player announced. "We don't have any information yet." I wondered how we were meant to gather information at any point in the agitated cross talk, but never mind. A regular named Barth was quickly exiled, on grounds of past performance—he'd proven such a generally deceptive player that he couldn't be trusted now. Roberta, who with her stature and chesty volume was strongly dominant in the village, led this charge. Barth succumbed to our lynch mob under groaning protest. "Night" fell, we "slept," and when day came again Adam announced that a woman named Kelly had been taken out by the mafia.

Kelly's murder drew shouts and giggles of surprise. Why had they picked her? Perhaps *this* was the information that would lead us to an informed lynching, instead of Barth's whimsical sacrifice. The village again plunged into an uproar of accusations and deflection. I turned to the woman beside me, a sylphlike girl with dyed-black shortish hair, who hadn't spoken. "Are you in the mafia?" I asked her, not quite whispering.

She blinked at me. "I'm a villager."

"Me too." I told her my name, and she told me hers— Doe. Our exchange was easily covered by the shouts of the village leadership, mainly Roberta Jar and a couple of strident men, as they led our next purge.

"First time?" Doe asked.

"Yes."

"That doesn't mean you aren't lying to me."

"No, it doesn't," I said. "But I'm not. Whom do you suspect?"

"I'm hopeless at this." Unashamed, she met my eye. I felt a pang. Doe was everything Roberta Jar was not: diminutive, vulnerable, and, I began to hope, single.

"We'll work together," I suggested. "Be watchful."

Mafia was a kind of fun, I decided. It elicited from us heaps of behavior: embarrassment and self-reproach, chummy consensus building that curdled at a moment's notice to feints of real paranoia and isolation, even measures of self-righteous, persecuted fury. The intensity was enthralling, but it was also strangely hollow, because it lacked any real content. For all the theatrics, we revealed nothing of ourselves, told no tales. It was that for which I yearned.

It was the morning of the third day that I fell under suspicion. Irrevocably, as it turned out. "I think we're ignoring the new people," said Roberta Jar. "I've seen it again and again, some newcomer draws the mafia card and sits there, playing innocent and silent, just mowing the village down while we argue. I think we ought to look at Joel, for instance. He isn't saying *anything*."

"I heard him talking to Doe," someone volunteered. "They have some little thing going on the side."

"Both mafia, then," said one of the leader men, whose every pronouncement was full of unearned certainty. "Take them both out."

"I'm a villager," I said. This was the standard protest, despite its deep meaninglessness: Who wouldn't say that?

Someone laughed at me sharply for being unpersuasive. Before I'd assembled a better defense, hands shot up all around the circle. Even Doe voted for my banishment.

Adam Cressner then shepherded the village into night. "The dead usually wander off where they can talk without disturbing the village," he stage-whispered across their bowed heads. I took the hint. As I moved into the hall, Adam returned to narration: "Mafia, open your eyes, and silently agree on someone to kill—" I wondered who the dastards were.

The zombies who'd vacated the parlor were gathered out on the brownstone's stoop, smoking cigarettes and gabbling. They spotted me peering through the front door's doubled glass panes. I made a gesture meant to be interpretable as *Be right there, just going for a pee.* Someone waved back. I went downstairs.

The half-basement's front room was furnished as a suburban den, with a stereo and large-screen TV, and walls lined with CDs, laser discs, and books, many of them expensive museum catalogues, compendiums of film stills, photo-essays from boutique imprints. I spotted a brightly colored paperback on a shelf of oversized volumes on art and antiquities: *Origins*, by Stan Lee, a reprint compendium of comic books introducing various Marvel characters: Spider-Man, Iron Man, the Fantastic Four. A sequel, *Son of Origins*, was shelved beside it. I browsed both, but the Vision wasn't included. He wasn't the sort of character who'd had such a prominent debut—more of a cult figure, I recalled. Like Rhoda or Fraser, he'd been an unplanned star, spun from an ensemble.

The pop-art panels looked thin and fraudulent on white paper, instead of the soft, yellowed rag of the old comics from which they'd been reprinted. Nevertheless, I felt a howling nostalgia rise in me at the sight of the Silver Surfer and Daredevil, characters who'd meant a tremendous amount to me for a brief moment in junior high, then been utterly forgotten. I'd discovered Marvel Comics a year or two after leaving P.S. 29 and Adam Cressner behind. The oddness of Adam's choice in identifying with the Vision had had a troubling chicken-or-egg quality to me then—did the character seem so depressed and diffident to me *because* of Adam's red face paint? The answer wasn't in *Origins*, or *Son of Origins*.

I replaced the books on the shelf and went digging in the walk-in closet instead.

"Hello?" Someone had entered the room behind me. It was Doe, swinging a beer bottle elegantly by the neck.

"Oh, hi," I said.

"What are you doing?"

"Looking for something."

"Something?"

"A costume, or a cape," I said. "It's a long story." I emerged from the closet, which seemed to hold only wool coats and ski gear anyway. "Did you get voted out of the village?"

"Right after you."

"Sorry. I guess I dragged us both down with that suspicious side talk. A rookie mistake."

"It's okay. They were right to. I was in the mafia."

"Ah. Now I feel truly foolish."

"Don't. It was brave of you to speak up at all. The first time I played I just cowered." Her tiny mouth was perfect apart from one incisor that seemed to have been inserted sideways for variation, like a domino.

"How do you know Adam and Roberta?"

"Adam was my dissertation adviser. At Columbia." Doe squinted at me oddly, expectantly, perhaps sensing I didn't know the first thing about Adam. She was right and wrong, of course.

"I'm just the friendly neighbor," I said. I considered how the word *friendly* could mean *not an actual friend*— like friendish, or friendlike. "Is this a whole, ah, Columbia group, upstairs?" I wondered what the man who'd been the Vision would teach: Android identity politics?

"Just that guy Barth who got killed. The rest I don't know. Adam and Roberta seem to collect people from all over the place."

"They're not big on introductions, are they? They prefer keeping everyone in the dark, and dependent on them."

"Maybe they figure we're grown-ups and can take care of ourselves."

I'd touched the limits of Doe's disloyalty, and been admonished. I rather liked it. "Yes, of course," I agreed. "The way we are, now, for instance. You and I, I mean. Taking care of ourselves."

Doe only blinked, as when, in the circle upstairs, I'd probed her mafia status.

There commenced a clunking and scraping of chairs above our heads. The village had shrunk, or dissolved. I stepped forward and took Doe's hand, thinking I only had a minute. I had less, as it happened. For a giantess Roberta Jar moved silently, and now she was in the doorway. Doe's hand slipped from mine as a newt darts from view on a forest path.

"Game over?" I asked.

"Yes," said Roberta, cat-ate-canaryishly. "The mafia won."

"The mafia always wins," said Doe, a little petulantly, I thought, given her own affiliation.

"Not really," said Roberta. "But they have had their way recently, it's true."

"They did fine without *my* help," mused Doe. This accounted for her bitterness: she'd wanted to prove essential.

We returned upstairs on a quest for more beer. The smokers had returned from the stoop, and villagers and mafia alike mingled in excited dissection of the game's plot: *I told you so* was the general thrust. There was hopeful talk of another game, but Val and Irene, a couple with babysitter problems, had to go. A few more defections followed, and suddenly we didn't have numbers enough for a village. "Don't everybody go," said Adam, as one after another made their excuses. "The night is young."

Seven of us remained. Happily, this included Doe. There were also two younger men vying for the attention of an Asian woman named Flour. Perhaps predictably, it was singles who'd stayed—us with nothing to rush home to. We sat in the sea of empty bottles and abandoned chairs, a ghost village. But Adam Cressner and Roberta Jar seemed glad to have us. He went downstairs and soon Chet Baker emanated from speakers in the parlor's corners. Roberta lowered the lights.

"I know a game," I said.

"Yes?" said Roberta.

"It's called I Never. It's a drinking game, though. We all have to have an alcoholic beverage in our hands."

Adam plopped two fresh sixes of Pale Ale at our feet. I explained the rules: Each of us in turn made a statement— a true statement—beginning with the words *I never.* Those in the circle who'd done the things the speaker hadn't were required to confess their experience, by sipping their beer. Thus the worldly among us were made to grow embarrassed, and intoxicated, and thus secrets were flushed into the open.

"For example, I'll start," I said. "I've never had sex on an airplane."

Adam and Roberta smiled at one another and tipped their bottles. Flour also wet her lips, and one of her suitors as well. Doe and the second of Flour's men were in my more innocent camp.

"Excellent," I said. "The rest is just a matter of thinking of good questions." I felt now an unexpectedly sharp appetite for this game—I wanted Adam and Roberta, and Doe too, to see how false the drama of Mafia was compared to our real lives. Of course, after my example we first had to endure a tentative round of inquiries into sex on trains, in restaurant coatrooms, in film projection booths, etc. When my turn came again I ratcheted things up a notch.

"I've never had sex with anyone in this room," I said.

Adam and Roberta clinked bottles, toasting smug coupledom.

Then Doe raised her drink and gulped, eyes closed. "*Oooh*," said one of the single men. I did the easy math, then inspected Roberta for her reaction. If anything, she looked ready to toast Doe's confession as well. Certainly it came as no surprise.

"I've . . . never . . ." Flour thought hard, eager to fill the loud silence. We were eager to have her fill it. "I've . . . never . . . had sex with a married person."

"Good one," congratulated one of her suitors.

I was forced to drink to this, as were our sybaritic hosts—and, yes, Doe. Her long-lashed eyes remained cast down to the floor, or squeezed as if in pain.

It was Adam's turn. "I've never killed anything bigger than a cockroach," he said.

Neither had I. Nor Roberta Jar, nor the woman named Flour or her two wannabe boyfriends. No, it was Doe again who had been trapped by the odd question, who raised her bottle once more to her thin-pressed lips. I wasn't sure she actually drank, but I wasn't about to call her on it.

It's the nature of I Never, as in other of life's arenas,

that though explanations aren't called for in the rules one often feels compelled to explain. I can't claim our circle didn't look to Doe for some gloss on her lonely confession.

"I was five," she began, and there was something ominous in the specificity: not *four or five*, or *five or six*. "My uncle had given me a new kitten, and I was playing alone in the yard with it, with some string. I hadn't even given the kitten a name yet." Doe looked at Adam Cressner, as if the whole game had devolved to the authority of his eerie question. "There was a tree in the yard, it's still there"—she spoke as though hypnotized, and seeing the tree float before her—"my parents still have the house. I used to climb the tree, and I had the idea I would take the kitten up the tree with me. I tied the string around the kitten's neck"—here Flour gasped—"and tried to pulley it up with me, across a branch."

Her tale's Clint Eastwoodian climax having been telegraphed by Adam's question, Doe was permitted a graceful elision. "A neighbor saw the whole thing from a window across the yard. He thought I'd done it on purpose, and he told my parents."

"Did they believe you?" asked Roberta Jar, clinically impassive.

"I don't know," said Doe, raising her eyebrows. "It didn't matter, really. Every since then I think something broke inside me . . . when my parents made me understand that the kitten wasn't alive anymore . . . there's always been a part of me missing."

"That's *horrible*," said one of Flour's men.

"I mean, I still have a capacity for happiness," said Doe, matter-of-factly, almost impatiently. It was as though she wanted to protect us from her story now, felt bad for telling it.

We meditated in silence on what we'd learned. Someone guzzled their beer, not as a gesture within the game, just to do it: a quiet pop of bottle mouth unsealing from lips was audible in a break between songs, Chet Baker finishing "I Fall in Love Too Easily," then, absurdly, beginning "Everything Happens to Me." I'd have been tempted to put my arm around Doe's shoulders, or even lead her from the room, if she as much as met my eye. She didn't. Tears streaked Flour's ivory cheeks instead.

Adam Cressner began speaking. At first it seemed a hollow gambit, an attempt to distract us from Doe's testimony by non sequitur. "When I was last in Germany, I visited the Glyptotek in Munich," he said. "It's full of statuary the Europeans ripped out of the old temples. They've got a Roman copy of a Greek marble by Boëthus—the original's in the Vatican—showing a boy with a goose. The bird's practically as big as the boy, and they're wrestling. The kid's got the goose by the neck. A museum guard came up behind me, he saw I was transfixed by this sculpture, and he uttered this line I'll never forget, it shot through me like a bolt: 'Spielend, doch, mit toedlichem Griff.' *He thinks it's a game, but he's choking the goose.* But in the guard's High German it was more allusive and grand—'playing, but with a deadly grip.' "

"Like something from Rilke," said Roberta Jar.

Oh yes, I thought viciously, *Rilke* and *High German* after four or five beers. You're both such fine people. However slow my uptake, a picture formed: I now supposed Doe's dissertation had been in art history, for example. And that Adam Cressner and Roberta Jar had together known, from intimate experience, how easily Doe might be induced to turn herself inside out for us.

I wanted revenge on Doe's behalf. "I've never," I said loudly.

All stared. I began again. "I've never pretended I was a character from a comic book. Never, say, dressed up in a superhero costume, not even on Halloween." I glared at Adam Cressner: Let him eat cape.

It was Roberta Jar who drew our attention, though, by lifting her bottle high, as if to toast again before she sipped. We looked to her as we had to Doe.

"I met a man once," Roberta said. "I liked this man, well, very, very much. This was eight years ago now." She lolled her big head, a little shy to tell it, though her voice was still strong and resonant in her chest. "When we began to see one another, this man and I, there was something between us that was difficult, a secret—a secret priority in his life. It had to do with this, exactly: dressing up as a character from a comic book. And this priority was difficult for both of us."

She'd turned my hostile joke into another confession, to give Doe company. We listened wide-eyed—I caught Flour glancing at me, likely wondering how I'd known to ask the question, as I'd wondered before at Adam Cressner. As for Adam, he sat quietly adoring his paramour while she spilled on.

"I realized I had to learn as much about this as I could, or it would beat us, and I was determined not to be beaten. I discovered that the comic-book character in question had gotten married, to another character, called the Scarlet Witch. I thought this was very unusual, two married superheroes, and I took it as a good sign. So, I went shopping for fabric, and hand-sewed a Scarlet Witch costume. Tights, and pink boots, a sort of pink headpiece to hold back my hair. I did a good job, really impressed myself. It was the most sustained arts-and-crafts project of my life, actually."

Roberta paused, and in the silence we were allowed to sense the result of her efforts, a climax as inevitable and in its way as horrible as the kitten's execution. I wondered if Adam still wore the red food coloring for face paint, or whether he'd found some better method, easier to remove when he'd wanted to pass for a mere Columbia professor. I thought of the Scarlet Witch as I knew her from Marvel Comics, an exotic beauty whose powers, loosely defined as "sorcery," mostly consisted of throwing up pink force fields, but whose real achievement was a stoical, unwavering devotion to her Spock-like emotional mute of a husband.

I looked again to Adam Cressner. I still faintly wished for the satisfaction of an unmasking, but his eyes gave me nothing. Adam Cressner was as little interested in my impressions of his Visionhood as he'd been at second base, all those years ago. He hadn't even sipped his beer to confess the truth.

"I have to go," said Doe suddenly. She flinched her head from me, from all of us, hastily gathered a load of beer bottles into the kitchen and rinsed them in the sink. I wondered if she'd also been enticed into a costume—Ant-Girl, or Thumbelina.

"Well, anyway, that's my story," said Roberta, the sardonic twang restored to her voice. One of the men gave an artificial laugh, barely adequate to break the tension. It was only now that Adam Cressner followed the game's protocol and also drank. I'd had my answer, though not as I'd wanted it, from Adam's mouth. I don't even know whether Flour or the two men had any understanding of what had happened—for all Roberta had told us, the man in question could have been someone other than Adam. Strangely, it was as if he and I were allies, having each forced confession from the other's woman. Except that neither woman was mine, and both might be his.

"A beautiful story it is," said Adam Cressner. "With that we'll see our dear guests to the door, yes?"

No one resisted. The spell was broken. *We* were in some way broken, shattered by the game, unable to recover any sense of delight in one another's company, if we'd ever had that—I no longer knew. We cleared bottles, shuffled chairs, mumbled excuses, made promises to be in touch, to forward one another's e-mail addresses, which rang hollow. Within ten minutes we were out on the street, each headed home alone. At least I think we were alone. Certainly Doe strolled away, apart from the others, a tiny figure vanishing on the pavement, before I'd turned my back and descended into my basement entrance, before I'd even had a chance to wish her good night or kiss her equivocally on the cheek. It's possible one of Flour's suitors followed her home, but I doubt it. It had all been a little much for us poor singles, the tyranny of the Vision and the Scarlet Witch.

Access Fantasy

THERE WAS A START-UP ABOUT A HALF MILE ahead the day before, a fever of distant engines and horns honking as others signaled their excitement—a chance to move!—and so he'd spent the day jammed behind the wheel, living in his Apartment on Tape, waiting for that chance, listening under the drone of distant helicopters to hear the start-up make its way downtown. But the wave of revving engines stalled before reaching his street. He never even saw a car move, just heard them. In fact he couldn't remember seeing a car move recently. Perhaps the start-up was only a panic begun by someone warming their motor, reviving their battery. That night he'd dreamed another

start-up, or perhaps it was real, a far-off flare that died before he'd even ground the sleep out of his eyes, though in
the rustle of his waking thoughts it was a perfect thing, co-
ordinated, a dance of cars shifting through the free-
flowing streets. Dream or not, either way, didn't matter.
He fell back asleep. What woke him in the morning was
the family in the Pacer up ahead cooking breakfast. They
had a stove on the roof of their car and the dad was
grilling something they'd bought from the flatbed shep-
herd two blocks away, a sheepsteak or something. It
smelled good. Everything about the family in the Pacer
made him too conscious of his wants. The family's daughter—she was beautiful—had been working as Advertising,
pushing up against and through the One-Way Permeable
Barrier on behalf of some vast faceless corporation. That
being the only way through the One-Way Permeable Barrier, of course. So the family, her ma and pa, were flush,
had dough, and vendors knew to seek them out, hawking
groceries. Whereas checking his pockets he didn't have
more than a couple of dollars. There was a coffee-and-
doughnuts man threading his way through the traffic even
now but coffee was beyond his means. He needed money.
Rumors had it Welfare Helicopters had been sighted south
of East One Thousand, One Hundred and Ninety-Fourth
Street, and a lot of people had left their cars, drifted down
that way, looking for easy cash. Which was one reason the
start-up died, it occurred to him—too many empty cars.
Along with the cars that wouldn't start anymore, like the
old lady in the Impala beside him, the dodderer. She'd

given up, spent most days dozing in the backseat. Her nephew from a few blocks away came over and tinkered with her engine now and again but it wasn't helping. It just meant the nephew wasn't at his wheel for the start-up, another dead spot, another reason not to bother waiting to move. Probably he thought now he should have walked downtown himself in search of welfare money drifting down from the sky. The state helicopters weren't coming around this neighborhood much lately. Alas. The air was crowded with commercial hovercraft instead, recruiters, Advertising robots rounding up the girl from the Pacer and others like her, off to the world on the other side of the One-Way Permeable Barrier, however briefly. The world of apartments, real ones. Though it was morning he went back to his latest Apartment on Tape, which was a four-bedroom two-bath co-op on East One Thousand, Two Hundred and Fifteenth Street, just a few blocks away but another world of course, remote from his life on the street, sealed off from it by the One-Way Permeable Barrier. He preferred the early part of the tape, before any of the fur-nishings arrived, so he rewound to that part and put the tape on slow and lived in the rooms as hard as he could, ignoring the glare of sun through his windshield that dulled his view of the dashboard television, ignoring the activities of the family in the Pacer up ahead as they clam-bered in and out of the hatchback, ignoring the clamor of his own pangs. The realtor's voice was annoying, it was a squawking, parroty voice so he kept the volume down as always and lived in the rooms silently, letting his mind sweep in and haunt the empty spaces, the rooms unfolding in slow motion for the realtor's camera. While the camera lingered in the bathroom he felt under his seat for his bottle and unzipped and peed, timed so it matched to the close-up of the automatic flushing of the toilet on his television. Then the camera and his attention wandered out into the hall. That's when he noticed it, the shadow. Just for a moment. He rewound to see it again. On the far wall of the hallway, framed perfectly for an instant in the lens, was the silhouette of a struggle, a man with his hands on the neck of another, smaller. A woman. Shaking her by the neck for that instant, before the image vanished. Like a pantomime of murder, a Punch-and-Judy show hidden in the Apartment on Tape. But real, it had to be real. Why hadn't he noticed before? He'd watched this tape dozens of times. He rewound again. Just barely, but still. Unmistakable, however brief. The savagery of it was awful. If only he could watch it frame by frame—slow motion was disastrously fast now. Who was the killer? The landlord? The realtor? Why? Was the victim the previous tenant? Questions, he had questions. He felt himself begin to buzz with them, come alive. Slow motion didn't seem particularly slow precisely because his attention had quickened. Yes, a job of detection was just what he needed to roust himself out of the current slump, burn off the torpor of too many days locked in the jam at the same damn intersection— why hadn't he gone downtown at that last turnoff, months ago? Well, anyway. He watched it again, memorized the shadow, the silhouette, imagined blurred features in the slurry of video fuzz, memorized the features, what the hell. Like a police sketch, work from his own prescient hallucinations. Again. It grew sharper every time. He'd scrape a hole in this patch of tape, he knew, if he rewound too many times. Better to have the tape, the evidence, all there was at this point. He popped the video, threw it in a satchel with notebook, eyeglasses. Extra socks. Outside, locked the car, tipped an imaginary hat at the old lady, headed east by foot on West One Thousand, Two Hundred and Eighth Street. He had to duck uptown two blocks to avoid a flotilla of Sanitation hovertrucks spraying foamy water to wash cars sealed up tight against this artificial rain but also soaking poor jerks asleep, drenching interiors, the rotted upholstery and split spongy dashboards, extinguishing rooftop bonfires, destroying box gardens, soap bubbles poisoning the feeble sprouts. Children screamed and giggled, the streets ran with water, sluicing shit here and there into drains, more often along under the tires to the unfortunate neighboring blocks, everyone moaning and lifting their feet clear. Just moving it around, that's all. At the next corner he ran into a crowd gathered staring at a couple of young teenage girls from inside, from the apartments, the other side of the barrier. They'd come out of the apartment building on rollerblades to sightsee, to slum on the streets. Sealed in a murky bubble of the One-Way Permeable Barrier they were like apparitions, dim ghosts, though you could hear them giggle as they skated through the hushed, reverent crowd. Like a sighting of gods, these teenage girls from inside. No one bothered to spare-change them or bother them in any way because of the barrier. The girls of course were oblivious behind their twilight veil, like night things come into the day, though for them probably it was the people in cars and around the cars that appeared dim, unreachable. He shouldered his way through the dumbstruck crowd and once past this obstacle he found his man, locked into traffic like all the rest, right where he'd last seen him. The Apartments on Tape dealer, his connection, sunbathing in a deck chair on the roof of his Sentra, eating a sandwich. The backseat was stacked with realtors' tapes, apartment porn, and on the passenger seat two video decks for dubbing. His car in a sliver of morning sun that shone across the middle of the block, benefit of a chink in the canyon of towers that surrounded them. The dealer's neighbors were on their car roofs as well, stretching in the sun, drying clothes. "Hello there, remember me? That looks good what you're eating, anyway, I want to talk to you about this tape." "No refunds," said the dealer, not even looking down. "No, that's not it, I saw something, can we watch it together?" "No need since there's no refunds and I'm hardly interested—" "Listen, this is a police matter, I think—" "You're police then, is that what you're saying?" still not looking down. "No no, I fancy myself a private detective, though not to say I work outside the law, more adjacent, then turn it over to them if it serves justice, there's so often corruption—" "So turn it over," the dealer said. "Well if you could just have a look I'd value your opinion. Sort of pick your brain," thinking flattery or threats, should have chosen one approach with this guy, stuck with it. The dealer said, "Sorry, day off," still not turning his head, chewing off another corner of sandwich. Something from inside the sandwich fell, a chunk of something, fish maybe, onto the roof of the car. "The thing is I think I saw a murder, on the tape, in the apartment." "That's highly unlikely." "I know, but that's what I saw." "Murder, huh?" The dealer didn't sound at all impressed. "Bloody body parts, that sort of thing?" "No, don't be absurd, just a shadow, just a trace." "Hmmm." "You never would have noticed in passing. Hey, come to think of it, you don't have an extra sandwich do you?" "No, I don't. So would you describe this shadow as sort of a flicker then, like a malfunction?" "No, absolutely not. It's part of the tape." "Not your monitor on the fritz?" "No"—he was getting angry now—"a person, a shadow strangling another shadow." The chunk of sandwich filling on the car roof was sizzling slightly, changing color already in the sun. The dealer said, "Shadows, hmmm. Probably a gimmick, subliminal special effects or something." "What? What reason would a realtor have for adding special effects for God's sake to an apartment tape?" "Maybe they think it adds some kind of allure, some thrill of menace that makes their apartments stand out from the crowd." "I doubt very much—" "Maybe they've become aware of the black market in tapes lately, that's the word on the street in fact, and so they're trying to send a little message. They don't like us ogling their apartments, even vicariously." "You can't ogle vicariously,

I think. Sounds wrong. Anyway, that's the most ridiculous thing I've ever—" "Or maybe I'm in on it, maybe I'm the killer, have you considered that?" "Now you're making fun of me." "Why? If you can solve crimes on the other side of the barrier why can't I commit them?" The dealer laughed, hyena-like. "Now seriously," he continued, "if you want to exchange for one without a murder I'll give you a credit toward the next, half what you paid—" "No thanks. I'll hold on to it." Discouraged, hungry, but he couldn't really bother being angry. What help did he expect from the dealer anyway? This was a larger matter, above the head of a mere middleman. "Good luck, Sherlock," the dealer was saying. "Spread word freely, by the way, don't hold back. Can't hurt my sales any. People like murder, only it might be good if there was skin instead of only shadow, a tit say." "Yes, very good then, appreciate your help. Carry on." The dealer saluted. He saluted back, started off through the traffic, stomach growling, ignoring it, intent. A killer was at large. Weaving past kids terrorizing an entire block of cars with an elaborate tag game, cornering around the newly washed neighborhood now wringing itself out, muddy streams between the cars and crying babies ignoring vendors with items he couldn't afford and a flatbed farmer offering live kittens for pets or food and a pathetic miniature start-up, three cars idiotically nosing rocking jerking back and forth trying to rearrange themselves pointlessly, one of them now sideways wheels on the curb and nobody else even taking the bait he made his way back to his car and key in the lock noticed the girl from the

Pacer standing in her red dress on the hood of the car gazing skyward, waiting for the Advertising people to take her away. Looking just incidentally like a million bucks. Her kid brother was away, maybe part of the gang playing tag, and her parents were inside the car doing housework Dad scraping the grill out the window Mom airing clothes repacking bundles so he went over, suddenly inspired. "Margaret, isn't it?" She nodded, smiled. "Yes, good, well you remember me from next door, I'm looking for a day or two's work and do you think they'll take me along?" She said, "You never know, they just take you or they don't." Smiling graciously even if a little confused, neighbors so long and they'd never spoken. "But you always—" he began pointing out. She said, "Oh once they've started taking you then—" Awkwardly, they were both awkward for a moment not saying what they both knew or at least he did, that she was an attractive young girl and likely that made a huge difference in whether they wanted you. "Well you wouldn't mind if I tried?" he said and she said, "No, no," relieved almost, then added, "I can point you out, I can suggest to them—" Now he was embarrassed and said hurriedly, "That's so good of you, thanks, and where should I wait, not here with you at your folks' car, I guess—" "Why not, climb up." Dad looked out the door up at them and she waved him off. "It's okay, you know him from next door he's going to work, we're going to try to get him a job Advertising." "Okay, sweetheart, just checking on you." Then she grabbed his arm, said, "Look." The Advertising hovercraft she'd been watching for landed on the curb a half block ahead, near the giant hideous sculpture at an office building main entrance, lately sealed. Dad said, "Get going you guys, and good luck," and she said, "C'mon." Such neighborliness was a surprise since he'd always felt shut out by the family in the Pacer but obviously it was in his head. And Margaret, a cloud of good feeling seemed to cover her. No wonder they wanted her for Advertising. "Hurry," she said and took his hand and they hopped down and pushed their way around the cars and through the chaos of children and barking dogs and vendors trying to work the crowd of wannabes these landings always provoked, to join the confused throng at the entrance. He held on to his satchel with the video and his socks making sure it didn't get picked in this crowd. She bounced there trying to make herself visible until one of the two robots at the door noticed her and pointed. They stepped up. "Inside," said the robot. They were ugly little robots with their braincases undisguised and terrible attitudes. He disliked them instantly. "I brought someone new," she said, pulling him by the hand, thrusting him into view. "Yes, sir, I'd like to enlist—" he started, grinning madly, wanting to make a good impression. The robot looked him over and made its rapid-fire assessment, nodded. "Get inside," it said. "Lucky," she whispered, and they stepped into the hovercraft. Four others were there, two men, two women, all young. And another woman stumbled in behind them, and the door sealed, and they were off. Nasty little robots scurrying into the cockpit, making things ready. "Now what?"

he said and she put her finger to her lips and shushed him,
but sweetly, leaning into him as if to say they were in this
together. He wanted to tell her what he was after but the
robots might hear. Would they care? Yes, no, he couldn't
know. Such ugly, fascistic little robots. Nazi robots, that's
what they were. He hated placing himself in their hands.
But once he was Advertising he would be through the barrier, he'd be able to investigate. Probably he should keep
his assignment to himself, though. He didn't want to get
her into trouble. The hovercraft shuddered, groaned, then
lifted and through the window he could see the cars growing smaller, his neighborhood, his life, the way the traffic
was so bad for hundreds of miles of street and why did he
think a start-up would change anything? Was there a place
where cars really drove anymore? Well, anyway. The robots were coming around with the Advertising Patches
and everyone leaned their heads forward obediently, no
first-timers like himself apparently. He did the same. A robot fastened a patch behind his right ear, a moment of
stinging skin, nothing more. Hard to believe the patch was
enough to interfere with the function of the One-Way Permeable Barrier, that he would now be vivid and tangible
and effective to those on the other side. "I don't feel any
different," he whispered. "You won't," she said, "not until
there's people. Then you'll be compelled to Advertise. You
won't be able to help it." "For what, though?" "You never
know, coffee, diamonds, condoms, vacations, you just
never know." "Where—" "They'll drop us off at the Undermall, then we're on our own." "Will we be able to stick

together?" The question was out before he could wonder if it was presuming too much, but she said, "Sure, as long as our products aren't too incompatible, but we'll know soon. Anyway, just follow me." She really had a warmth, a glow. Incompatible products? Well, he'd find out what that meant. The hovercraft bumped down on the roof of a building, and with grim efficiency the ugly Nazi robots had the door open and were marching the conscripts out to a rooftop elevator. He wanted to reach out and smack their little exposed-braincase heads together. But he had to keep his cool, stay undercover. He trotted across the roof toward the elevator after her, between the rows of officious gesticulating robots, like they were going to a concentration camp. The last robot at the door of the elevator handed them each an envelope before they stepped in. He took his and moved into the corner with Margaret, they were really packing them in but he couldn't complain actually being jostled with her and she didn't seem to be trying to avoid it. He poked into the envelope. It was full of bills, singles mostly. The money was tattered and filthy, bills that had been taken out of circulation on the other side of the barrier. Garbage money, that's what it was. The others had already pocketed theirs, business as usual apparently. "Why do they pay us now?" he whispered. She said, "We just find our way out at the end, when the patch runs out, so this way they don't have to deal with us again," and he said, "What if we just took off with the money?" "You could I guess, but I've never seen anyone do it since you'd never get to come back and anyway the

patch makes you really want to Advertise, you'll see." Her
voice was reassuring, like she really wanted him not to
worry and he felt rotten not telling her about his investigation, his agenda. He put the envelope into his satchel
with tape and socks. The elevator sealed and whooshed
them down through the building, into the Undermall, then
the doors opened and they unpacked from the elevator,
spewed out into a gigantic lobby, all glass and polished
steel with music playing softly and escalators going down
and up in every direction, escalators with steps of burnished wood that looked good enough to eat, looked like
roast chicken. He was still so hungry. Margaret took his
hand again. "Let's go," she said. As the others dispersed
she led him toward one of the escalators and they descended. The corridor below branched to shops with recessed entrances, windows dark and smoky, quiet pulsing
music fading from each door, also food smells here and
there causing his saliva to flow, and holographic signs an-
gling into view as they passed: FERN SLAW, ROETHKE AND
SONS, HOLLOW APPEAL, BROKEN SMUDGED ALPHABET,
BURGER KING, PLASTIC DEVILS, OSTRICH LAKE, SMARTIN-
GALE'S, RED HARVEST, CATCH OF THE DAY, MUTUAL OF FO-
MALHAUT, THNEEDS, etcetera. She led him on, confidently,
obviously at home. Why not, this was what she did with
her days. Then without warning, a couple appeared from
around a corner, and he felt himself begin to Advertise.
"How do you do today?" he said, sidling up to the gentleman of the couple, even as he saw Margaret begin to do
the same thing to the lady. The gentleman nodded at him,

walked on. But met his eye. He was tangible, he could be heard. It was a shock. "Thirsty?" he heard himself say. "How long's it been since you had a nice refreshing beer?" "Don't like beer," said the gentleman. "Can't say why, just never have." "Then you've obviously never tried a Very Old Money Lager," he heard himself say, still astonished. The barrier was pierced and he was conversing, he was perceptible. He'd be able to conduct interrogations, be able to search out clues. Meanwhile he heard Margaret saying, "Don't demean your signature with a second-rate writing implement. Once you've tried the Eiger fountain pen you'll never want to go back to those henlike scratchings and scrawlings," and the woman seemed interested and so Margaret went on "our Empyrean Sterling Silver Collection features one-of-a-kind hand-etched casings—" In fact the man seemed captivated too. He turned ignoring the beer pitch and gave Margaret his attention. "Our brewers handpick the hops and malt," he was unable to stop though he'd obviously lost his mark, "and every single batch of fire-brewed Very Old Money Lager is individually tasted—" Following the couple through the corridor they bumped into another Advertising woman who'd been on the hovercraft, and she began singing, "Vis-it the *moon*, it's nev-er too *soon*," dancing sinuously and batting her eyes, distracting them all from fountain pens and beer for the moment and then the five of them swept into the larger space of the Undermall and suddenly there were dozens of people who needed to be told about the beer. "Thirsty? Hello, hi there, thirsty? Excuse me, thirsty? Yes?

Craving satisfaction, sparkle, bite? No? Yes? Have you tried Very Old Money? What makes it different, you ask— oh, hello, thirsty?" and also dozens of people working as Advertising, a gabble of pitches—stern, admonitory: "Have you considered the perils of being without success insurance?"; flippant, arbitrary: "You never know you're out with the Black Underwear Crowd, not until you get one of them home!"; jingly, singsong: "We've got children, we've all got children, you can have children too—" and as they scattered and darted along the endless marble floors of the Undermall he was afraid he'd lose her, but there was Margaret, earnestly discussing pens with a thoughtful older couple and he struggled over toward her, hawking beer—"Thirsty? Oof, sorry, uh, thirsty?" The crowd thinned as customers ducked into shops and stole away down corridors back to their apartments, bullied by the slew of Advertising except for the few like this older couple who seemed gratified by the attention, he actually had to wait as they listened and took down some information from Margaret about the Eiger fountain pen while he stood far enough away to keep from barking at them about the beer. Then once the older couple wandered off he took Margaret's hand this time, why not, she'd done it, and drew her down a corridor away from the crowds, hoping to keep from engaging with any more customers, and also in the right direction if he had his bearings. He thought he did. He led her into the shadow of a doorway, a shop called Fingertoes that wasn't doing much business. "Listen, I've got to tell you something, I haven't been completely truthful, I mean, I haven't lied, but there's something—" She looked at him, hopeful, confused, but generous in her interpretation, he could tell, what a pure and sweet disposition, maybe her dad wasn't such a bad guy after all if he'd raised a plum like this. "I'm a detective, I mean, what does that mean, really, but the thing is there's been a murder and I'm trying to look into it—" and then he plunged in and told all, the Apartment on Tape, pulling it out of his satchel to show her, the shadow, the strangling, his conversation with the dealer and then his brainstorm to slip inside the citadel, slip past the One-Way Permeable Barrier that would of course have kept his questions or accusations from even being audible to those on this side, and so he'd manipulated her generosity to get aboard the hovercraft. "Forgive me," he said. Her eyes widened, her voice grew hushed, reverent. "Of course, but what do you want to do? Find the police?" "You're not angry at me?" "No, no. It's a brave thing you're doing." "Thank you." They drew closer. He could almost kiss her, just in happiness, solidarity, no further meaning or if there was it was just on top of the powerful solidarity feeling, just an extra, a windfall. "But what do you think is best, the police?" she whispered. "No, I have in mind a visit to the apartment, we're only a couple of blocks away, in this direction I believe, but do you think we can get upstairs?" They fell silent then because a man swerved out of Fingertoes with a little paper tray of greasy fried things, looked like fingers or toes in fact and smelled terrific, he couldn't believe how hungry he was. "Thirsty?" he said hopelessly and the man popping one into his mouth said, "You called it, brother, I'm dying for a beer." "Why just any beer when you could enjoy a Very Old Money—" and he had to go on about it, being driven nuts by the smell, while Margaret waited. The moment the grease-eater realized they were Advertising and broke free, toward the open spaces of the Undermall, he and Margaret broke in the other direction, down the corridor. "This way," said Margaret, turning them toward the elevator, "the next level down you can go for blocks, it's the way out eventually too." "Yes, but can we get back upstairs?" "The elevators work for us until the patches run out, I think," and so they went down below the Undermall to the underground corridors, long echoey halls of tile, not so glamorous as upstairs, not nice at all really, the lengths apartment people went never to have to step out onto the street and see car people being really appalling sometimes. The tunnels were marked with street signs, names of other Undermalls, here and there an exit. They had to Advertise only once before reaching East One Thousand, Two Hundred and Fifteenth Street, to a group of teenage boys smoking a joint in the corridor who laughed and asked Margaret questions she couldn't answer like are they mightier or less mighty than the sword and do they work for pigs. They ran into another person Advertising, a man moving furtively who when he recognized Margaret was plainly relieved. "He's got a girlfriend," she explained, somewhat enigmatically. So those Advertising could, did—what? Interact. But caught up in the chase now, he didn't ask more, just counted the blocks, feeling the thrill of approaching his Apartment on Tape's real address. They went up in the elevator, which was lavish again, wood paneled and perfumed and mirrored and musical. An expensive building. Apartment 16D. So he pressed the button for the sixteenth floor, holding his breath, hardly believing it when they rose above the public floors. But they did. He gripped her hand. The elevator stopped on the sixth floor and a robot got on. Another of the creepily efficient braincase-showing kind. At first the robot ignored them but then on the fifteenth floor a woman got on and Margaret said, "The most personal thing about you is your signature, don't you think?" and he said, "Thirsty?" and the robot turned and stared up at them. The doors closed and they rode up to the sixteenth floor, and the three of them got out, he and Margaret and the robot, leaving the woman behind. The hallway was splendid with plush carpeting and brass light fixtures, empty apart from the three of them. "What are you doing up here?" said the robot. "And what's in that bag?" Clutching his satchel he said, "Nothing, just my stuff." "Why is it any of your business?" said Margaret, surprisingly defiant. "We've been asked to give an extended presentation at a customer's private home," he said, wanting quickly to cover Margaret's outburst, give the robot something else to focus on. "Then I'll escort you," said the robot. "You really don't have to do that," he said. "Don't come along and screw up our pitch, we'll sue you," Margaret added bizarrely. Learning of the investigation had an odd effect on her, always a risk working with amateurs he supposed. But also it was these robots, the way they were designed with rotten personalities or no personalities they really aroused revulsion in people, it was an instinctual thing and not just him, he noted with satisfaction. He squeezed her hand and said, "Our sponsors would be displeased, it's true." "This matter requires clearance," said the robot, trying to get in front of them as they walked, and they had to skip to stay ahead of it. "Please stand to one side and wait for clearance," but they kept going down the carpeted hallway, his fingers crossed that it was the right direction for 16D. "Halt," said the robot, a flashing red light on its forehead beginning to blink neurotically and then they were at the door, and he rapped with his knuckles, thinking, hardly going incognito here, but better learn what we can. "Stand to one side," said the robot again. "Shut up," said Margaret. As the robot clamped a steely hand on each of their arms, jerking them back away from the door, its treads grinding on the carpet for traction, probably leaving ugly marks too, the door swung open. "Hello?" The man in the doorway was unshaven and slack-haired wearing a robe and blinking at them as though he'd only turned on his light to answer the door. "They claim to have an appointment with you, sir," said the robot. The man only stood and stared. "It's very important, we have to talk to you urgently," he said, trying to pull free of the robot's chilly grip, then added, regretfully, "about beer." He felt a swoon at looking through the doorway, realizing he was seeing into his Apartment on Tape, the rooms etched into his dreamy brain now before

him. He tried to see more but the light was gloomy. "And
fountain pens," said Margaret, obviously trying to hold
herself back but compelled to chip in something. "I apologize, sir, I tried to detain them to obtain clearance—" said
the robot. *Detain, obtain,* what rotten syntax, he thought,
the people who program these robots certainly aren't
poets. The man just stood and blinked and looked them
over, the three of them struggling subtly, he and Margaret
trying to pull free of the robot, which was still blinking red
and grinding at the carpet. "Cooperate," squawked the robot. The man in the robe squinted at them, finally smiled.
"Please," said Margaret. "Fountain pens, eh?" the man in
the robe said at last. "Yes," said Margaret desperately,
and he heard himself add, "And beer—" "Yes, of course,"
mumbled the man in the robe. "How silly of me. Come
in." "Sir, for your safety—" "They're fine," said the man
to the robot. "I'm expecting them. Let them in." The robot released its grip. The man in the robe turned and shuffled inside. They followed him, all three of them, into
poorly lit rooms disastrously heaped with newspapers,
clothes, soiled dishes, empty and half-empty takeout packages, but still unmistakably the rooms from his tape, every
turn of his head recalling some camera movement and
there sure enough was the wall that had held the shadow,
the momentary stain of murder. The man in the robe
turned and said to the robot, "Please wait outside." "But
surely I should chaperone, sir—" "No, that's fine, just outside the door, I'll call you in if I need you. Close it on your
way out, thanks." Watching the robot slink back out he

couldn't help but feel a little thrill of vindication. The man
in the robe continued into the kitchen, and gesturing at the
table said, "Please, sit, sorry for the mess. Did you say
you'd like a beer?" "Well, uh, no, that wasn't exactly—if
you drink beer you ought to make it a Very Old Money
Lager for full satisfaction—but I've got something else to
discuss while you enjoy your delicious, oh, damn it—"
"Relax, have a seat. Can I get you something else?"
"Food," he blurted. "Which always goes best with a Very
Old Money," and meanwhile Margaret released his hand
and took a seat and started in talking about pens. The
man opened his refrigerator, which was as overloaded as
the apartment, another image from the tape now corrupted by squalor. "You poor people, stuck with those awful patches and yet I suppose I wouldn't have the benefit of
your company today without them! Ah, well. Here, I
wasn't expecting visitors but would you like some cheese?
Can I fix you a glass of water?" The man set out a crum-
bled hunk of cheddar with a butter knife, crumbs on the
dish and so long uncovered the edges were dried a deep,
translucent orange. "So, you were just Advertising and you
thought you'd pay a house call? How am I so lucky?"
"Well, that's not it exactly—" Margaret took the knife and
began paring away the edges of the cheese, carving out a
chunk that looked more or less edible and when she
handed it to him he couldn't resist, but tried talking
through the mouthful anyway, desperately trying to nego-
tiate the three priorities of hunger, Advertising, and his investigation: "Would you consider, mmmpphh, excuse me,

consider opening a nice tall bottle of Very Old Money and settling in to watch this videotape I brought with me because there's something I'd like you to see, a question I've got about it—" The man in the robe nodded absently, half listening, staring oddly at Margaret and then said, "By all means let me see your tape—is it about beer? I'd be delighted but no hurry, please relax and enjoy yourselves, I'll be right out," and stepped into the living room, began rummaging among his possessions of which there certainly were plenty. It was a little depressing how full the once glorious apartment had gotten. Margaret cut him another piece of cheese and whispered, "Do you think he knows something?" "I can't know he seems so nice, well if not nice then harmless, hapless, but I'll judge his reaction to the video, watch him closely when the time comes—" grabbing more cheese quickly while he could and then the man in the robe was back. "Hello, friends, enjoying yourselves?" His robe had fallen open and they both stared but maybe it was just an example of his sloppiness. Certainly there was no polite way to mention it. There was something confusing about this man, who now went to the table and took the knife out of Margaret's hands and held her hand there for a moment and then snapped something—was it a bracelet?—around her wrist. Not a bracelet. Handcuffs. "Hey, wait a minute, that's no way to enjoy a nice glass of lager!" he heard himself say idiotically cheese falling out of his mouth jumping up as the man clicked Margaret's other wrist into the cuffs and he had her linked to the back of her chair. He stood to intervene and the man in the robe swept his feet out from under him with a kick and pushed him in the chest and he fell, feet sliding on papers, hand skidding in lumps of cheese, to the floor. "Thirsty!" he shouted, the more excited the more fervent the Advertising, apparently. "No! Beer!" as he struggled to get up. And Margaret was saying something desperate about Eiger fountain pens "—*self-refilling cartridge*—" The man in the robe moved quickly, not lazy and sloppy at all now and kicked away his satchel with the tape inside and bent over him and reached behind his ear to tear the patch away, another momentary sting. He could only shout "Beer!" once more before the twilight world of the One-Way Permeable Barrier surrounded him, it was everywhere here, even Margaret was on the other side as long as she wore the patch, and he felt his voice sucked away to a scream audible inside the space of his own head but not elsewhere, he knew, not until he was back outside, on the street where he belonged and why couldn't he have stayed there? What was he thinking? Anyway it wouldn't be long now because through the gauze he saw the man in the robe who you'd have to call the man half out of his robe now open the door to let the robot in, then as the naked man grinned at him steel pinchers clamped onto his arm and he was dragged out of the room, screaming inaudibly, thrashing to no purpose, leaving Margaret behind. And his tape besides.

The Spray

THE APARTMENT WAS BURGLED AND THE police came. Four of them and a dog. The three youngest were like boys. They wore buzzing squawking radios on their belts. The oldest was in charge and the young ones did what he told them. The dog sat. They asked what was taken and we said we weren't sure—the television and the fax machine, at least. One of them was writing, taking down what we said. He had a tic, an eye that kept blinking. "What else?" the oldest policeman said. We didn't know what else. That's when they brought it out, a small unmarked canister, and began spraying around the house. First they put a mask over the mouth and nose of the dog.

None of them wore a mask. They didn't offer us any protection. Just the dog. "Stand back," they said. They sprayed in a circle toward the edges of the room. We stood clustered with the policemen. "What's that?" we said. "Spray," said the oldest policeman. "Makes lost things visible."

The spray settled like a small rain through the house and afterward glowing in various spots were the things the burglar had taken. It was a salmon-colored glow. On the table was a salmon-colored image of a box, a jewelry box that Addie's mother had given us. There was a salmon-colored glowing television and fax machine in place of the missing ones. On the shelves the spray showed a Walkman and a camera and a pair of cuff links, salmon-colored and luminous. In the bedroom was Addie's vibrator, glowing like a fuel rod. We all walked around the apartment, looking for things. The eye-tic policeman wrote down the names of the items that appeared. Addie called the vibrator a massager. The dog in the mask, eyes watering. I couldn't smell the spray. "How long does it last?" we said.

"About a day," said the policeman who'd done the spraying, not the oldest. "You know you c-can't use this stuff anymore, even though you c-can see it," he said. "It's gone."

"Try and touch it," said the oldest policeman. He pointed at the glowing jewelry box.

We did and it wasn't there. Our hands passed through the visible missing objects.

They asked us about our neighbors. We told them we

trusted everyone in the building. They looked at the fire escape. The dog sneezed. They took some pictures. The burglars had come through the window. Addie put a book on the bedside table on top of the glowing vibrator. It showed through, like it was projected onto the book. We asked if they wanted to dust for fingerprints. The older policeman shook his head. "They wore gloves," he said. "How do you know?" we said. "Rubber gloves leave residue, powder," he said. "That's what makes the dog sneeze." "Oh." They took more pictures. "Did you want something to drink?" The older one said no. One of the younger policemen said, "I'm allergic, just like the d-dog," and the other policemen laughed. Addie had a drink, a martini. The policemen shook our hands and then they went away. We'd been given a case number. The box and the cuff links and the rest still glowed. Then Addie saw that the policemen had left the spray.

She took the canister and said, "There was something wrong with those policemen."

"Do you mean how young they seemed?"

"No, I think they always look young. You just don't notice on the street. Outdoors you see the uniforms, but in the house you can see how they're just barely old enough to vote."

"What are you going to do with that?" I said.

She handled it. "Nothing. Didn't you think there was something strange about those policemen, though?"

"Do you mean the one with the lisp?"

"He didn't have a lisp, he had a twitchy eye."

"Well, there was one with an eye thing, but the one who stuttered—is that what you mean by strange?" Addie kept turning the canister over in her hands. "Why don't you let me take that," I said.

"It's okay," she said. "I guess I don't know what I mean. Just something about them. Maybe there were too many of them. Do you think they develop the pictures themselves, Aaron? Do they have a darkroom in the police station?"

I said, "Probably." She said, "Do you think the missing things show up in the photographs—the things the spray reveals?"

"Probably."

"Let's just keep it and see if they come back."

"I wish you would put it on the table, then."

"Let's find a place to hide it."

"They're probably doing some kind of inventory right now, at the police station. They'll probably be back for it any minute."

"So if we hide it—"

"If we hide it we look guiltier than if you just put it on the table."

"We didn't steal anything. Our house was broken into. They left it here."

"I wish you would put it on the table."

"I wonder if the police do their inventory by spraying around the police station to see what's missing?"

"So if we have their spray—"

"They'll never know what happened!" She shrieked with laughter. I laughed too. I moved next to her on the couch and we rolled and laughed like monkeys in a zoo. Still laughing, I put my hand on the spray canister. "Gimme," I said.

"Let go." Her laughter faded as she pulled at the can. The ends of several hairs were stuck to her tongue. I pulled on the can. And she pulled. We both pulled harder.

"Gimme," I said. I let go of the can and tickled her. "Gimme gimme gimme."

She grimaced and twisted away from me. "Not funny," she said.

"The police don't have their SPRAY!" I said, and kept tickling her.

"Not funny not funny." Slapping my hands away, she stood up.

"Okay. You're right, it's not funny. Put it on the table."

"Let's return it like you said."

"I'm too tired. Let's just hide it. We can return it tomorrow."

"Okay, I'll hide it. Cover your eyes."

"Not hide-and-seek. We have to agree on a place. A locked place."

"What's the big deal? Let's just leave it on the table." She put it on the table, beside the salmon-colored glowing box. "Maybe somebody will break in and take it. Maybe the police will break in."

"You're a little mixed up, I'd say." I moved closer to the table.

"I'm just tired." She pretended to yawn. "What a day."

"I don't miss the stuff that was taken," I said.

"You don't?"

"I hate television and faxes. I hate this little jewelry box."

"See if you're still saying that tomorrow, when you can't see them anymore."

"I only care about you, you, you." I grabbed the canister of spray. She grabbed it too. "Let go," she said.

"You're all I love, you're all that matters to me," I said.

We wrestled for the can again. We fell onto the couch together.

"Let's just put it down on the table," said Addie. "Okay." "Let go." "You first." "No, at the same time." We put it on the table.

"Are you thinking what I'm thinking," she said.

"I don't know, probably."

"What are you thinking?"

"What you're thinking."

"I'm not thinking anything."

"Then I'm not either."

"Liar."

"It probably doesn't work that way," I said. "The police wouldn't have a thing like that. It isn't the same thing."

"So why not try."

"Don't."

"You said it wouldn't work."

"Just don't. It's toxic. You saw them cover the dog's mouth."

"They didn't cover themselves. Anyway, I asked them about that when you were in the other room. They said it was so you wouldn't see the stuff the dog ate that fell out of its mouth. Because the dog is a very sloppy eater. So the spray would show what it had been eating recently, around the mouth. It's disgusting, they said."

"Now you're the liar."

"Let's just see."

I jumped up. "If you spray me I'll spray you," I shouted. The spray hit me as I moved across the room. The wet mist fell behind me, like a parachute collapsing in the spot where I'd been, but enough got on me. An image of Lucinda formed, glowing and salmon-colored.

Lucinda was naked. Her hair was short, like when we were together. Her head lay on my shoulder, her arms were around my neck, and her body was across my front. My shirt and jacket. Her breasts were mashed against me, but I couldn't feel them. Her knee was across my legs. I jumped backward but she came with me, radiant and insubstantial. I turned my head to see her face. Her expression was peaceful, but her little salmon-colored eyelids were half open.

"Ha!" said Addie. "I told you it would work."

"GIVE ME THAT!" I lunged for the spray. Addie ducked. I grabbed her arm and pulled her with me onto the couch. Me and Addie and Lucinda were all there together, Lucinda placidly naked. As Addie and I wrestled for the spray we plunged through Lucinda's glowing body, her luminous arms and legs.

I got my hands on the spray canister. We both had our hands on it. Four hands covering the one can. Then it went off. One of us pressed the nozzle, I don't know who. It wasn't Lucinda, anyway.

As the spray settled over us Charles became visible, poised over Addie. He was naked, like Lucinda. His glowing shoulders and legs and ass were covered with glowing salmon hair, like the halo around a lightbulb. His mouth was open. His face was blurred, like he was a picture someone had taken while he was moving his face, saying something.

"There you go," I said. "You got what you wanted." "I didn't want anything," said Addie.

We put the spray on the table.

"How long did the police say it would last?" I said. I tried not to look at Lucinda. She was right beside my head.

"About twenty-four hours. What time is it?"

"It's late. I'm tired. The police didn't say twenty-four hours. About a day, they said."

"That's twenty-four hours."

"Probably they meant it's gone the next day."

"I don't think so."

I looked at the television. I looked at the cuff links. I looked at Charles's ass. "Probably the sunlight makes it wear off," I said.

"Maybe."

"Probably you can't see it in the dark, in complete darkness. Let's go to bed."

We went into the bedroom. All four of us. I took off my shoes and socks. "Probably it's just attached to our clothes. If I take off my clothes and leave them in the other room—"

"Try it."

I took off my pants and jacket. Lucinda was attached to me, not the clothes. Her bare salmon knee was across my bare legs. I started to take off my shirt. Addie looked at me. Lucinda's face was on my bare shoulder.

"Put your clothes back on," said Addie.

I put them back on. Addie left her clothes on. We lay on top of the covers in our clothes. Lucinda and Charles were on top of us. I didn't know where to put my hands. I wondered how Addie felt about Charles's blurred face, his open mouth. I was glad Lucinda wasn't blurred. "Turn off the light," I said. "We won't be able to see them in the dark."

Addie turned off the light. The room was dark. Charles and Lucinda glowed salmon above us. Glowing in the blackness with the vibrator on the side table and the luminous dial of my watch.

"Just close your eyes," I said to Addie.

"You close yours first," she said.

Vivian Relf

Paper lanterns with candles inside, their flames capering in imperceptible breezes, marked the steps of the walkway. Shadow and laughter spilled from the house above, while music shorn of all but its pulse made its way like ground fog across the eucalyptus-strewn lawn. Doran and Top and Evie and Miranda drifted up the stairs, into throngs smoking and kissing cheeks and elbowing one another on the porch and around the open front door. Doran saw the familiar girl there, just inside.

He squinted and smiled, to offer evidence he wasn't gawking. To convey what he felt: he recognized her. She blinked at him, and parted her mouth slightly, then nipped her lower lip. Top and Evie and Miranda pushed inside the kitchen, fighting their way to the drinks surely waiting on a counter or in the refrigerator, but Doran hung back. He pointed a finger at the familiar girl, and moved nearer to her. She turned from her friends.

The foyer was lit with strings of red plastic chili peppers. They drooped in waves from the molding, their glow blushing cheeks, foreheads, ears, teeth.

"I know you from somewhere," he said.

"I was just thinking the same thing."

"You one of Jorn's friends?"

"Jorn who?"

"Never mind," said Doran. "This is supposed to be Jorn's house, I thought. I don't know why I even mentioned it, since I don't know him. Or her."

"My friends brought me," said the girl. "I don't even know whose party this is. I don't know if *they* know."

"My friends brought me too," said Doran. "Wait, do you waitress at Elision, on Dunmarket?"

"I don't live here. I must know you from somewhere else."

"Definitely, you look really familiar."

They were yelling to be heard in the jostle of bodies inside the door. Doran gestured over their heads, outside. "Do you want to go where we can talk?"

They turned the corner, stopped in a glade just short of the deck, which was as full of revelers as the kitchen and foyer. They nestled in the darkness between pools of light and chatter. The girl had a drink, red wine in a plastic cup. Doran felt a little bare without anything.

"This'll drive me crazy until I figure it out," he said. "Where'd you go to college?"

"Sundstrom," she said.

"I went to Vagary." Doran swallowed the syllables, knowing it was a confession: *I'm one of those Vagary types.* "But I used to know a guy who went to Sundstrom. How old are you?"

"Twenty-six."

"I'm twenty-eight. You would have been there at the same time." This was hardly a promising avenue. But he persisted. "Gilly Noman, that ring a bell?"

"Sounds like a girl's name."

"I know, never mind. Where do you live?"

She mentioned a city, a place he'd never been.

"That's no help. How long have you lived there?"

"Since college. Five years, I guess."

"Where'd you grow up?"

The city she mentioned was another cipher, a destination never remotely considered.

"Your whole life?" he asked. Doran racked his brain, but he didn't know anyone from the place.

"Yeah," she said, a bit defensively. "What about you?"

"Right here, right around here. Wait, this is ridiculous. You look so familiar."

"So do you." She didn't sound too discouraged.

"Who are your friends here?"

"Ben and Malorie. You know them?"

"No, but do you maybe visit them often?"

"First time."

"You didn't, uh, go to Camp Drewsmore, did you?" Doran watched how his feelings about the girl changed, like light through a turned prism, as he tried to fit his bodily certainty of her familiarity into each proposed context. Summer camp, for instance, forced him to consider whether she'd witnessed ball-field humiliations, or kissed one of the older boys who were his idol then, he, in his innocence, not having yet kissed anyone.

"No."

"Drewsmore-in-the-Mist?"

"Didn't go to camp."

"Okay, wait, forget camp, it must be something more recent. What do you do?"

"Until just now I worked on Congressman Goshen's campaign. We, uh, lost. So I'm sort of between things. What do you do?"

"Totally unrelated in every way. I'm an artist's assistant. Heard of London Jerkins?"

"No."

"To describe it briefly there's this bright purple zigzag in all his paintings, kind of a signature shape. I paint it." He mimed the movements, the flourish at the end. "By now I do it better than him. You travel a lot for the congressman thing?"

"Not ever. I basically designed his pamphlets and door hangers."

"Ah, our jobs aren't so different after all."

"But I don't have one now." She aped his zigzag flourish, as punctuation.

"Hence you're crashing parties in distant cities which happen to be where I live."

"Hey, you didn't even know if Jorn was a guy or a girl. I at least was introduced, though I didn't catch his name."

He put up his hands: no slight intended. "But where do I know you from? I mean, no pressure, but this is mutual, right? You recognize me too."

"I was sure when you walked in. Now I'm not so sure."

"Yeah, maybe you look a little less familiar yourself."

In the grade of woods over the girl's shoulder Doran sighted two pale copper orbs, flat as coins. Fox? Bunny? Raccoon? He motioned for the girl to turn and see, when at that moment Top approached them from around the corner of the house. Doran's hand fell, words died on his lips. Tiny hands or feet scrabbled urgently in the underbrush, as though they were repairing a watch. The noise vanished.

Top had his own cup of wine, half empty. Lipstick smudged his cheek. Doran moved to wipe it off, but Top bobbed, ducking Doran's reach. He glared. "Where'd you go?" he asked Doran, only nodding his chin at the familiar girl.

"We were trying to figure out where we knew each other from," said Doran. "This is my friend Top. I'm sorry, what's your name?"

"Vivian."

"Vivian, Top. And I'm Doran."

"Hello, Vivian," said Top, curtly, raising his cup. To Doran: "You coming inside?"

"Sure, in a minute."

Top raised his eyebrows, said: "Sure. Anyway, we'll be there. Me and Evie and Miranda." To Vivian: "Nice to meet you." He slipped around the corner again.

"Friends waiting for you?" said Vivian.

"Sure, I guess. Yours?"

"It's not the same. They're a couple."

"Letting you mingle, I guess that's what you mean."

"Whereas yours are what—dates?"

"Good question. It's unclear, though. I'd have to admit they're maybe dates. But only maybe. Vivian what?"

"Relf."

"Vivian Relf. Totally unfamiliar. I'm Doran Close. In case that triggers any recall." Doran felt irritable, reluctant to let go of it, possibly humiliated, in need of a drink.

"It doesn't."

"Have we pretty much eliminated everything?"

"I can't think of anything else."

"We've never been in any of the same cities or schools or anything at the same time." It gave him a queasy, earth-shifty sensation. As though he'd come through the door of the party wrong, on the wrong foot. Planted a foot or flag on the wrong planet: one small step from the foyer, one giant plunge into the abyss.

"Nope, I don't think so."

"You're not on television?"

"Never."

"So what's the basis of all this howling familiarity?"

"I don't know if there really is any basis, and anyway I'm not feeling such howling familiarity anymore."

"Right, me neither." This was now a matter of pure vertigo, cliff-side terror. He didn't hold it against Vivian Relf, though. She was his fellow sufferer. It was what they had in common, the sole thing.

"You want to go back to your friends?" she said.

"I guess so."

"Don't feel bad."

"I don't," lied Doran.

"Maybe I'll see you around."

"Very good then, Less-Than-Familiar-Girl. I'll look forward to that." Doran offered his hand to shake, mock-pompously. He felt garbed in awkwardness.

Vivian Relf accepted his hand, and they shook. She'd grown a little sulky herself, at the last minute.

Doran found Top and Evie and Miranda beyond the kitchen, in a room darkened and lit only by a string of Christmas lights, and cleared of all but two enormous speakers, as though for dancing. No one danced, no one inhabited the room apart from the three of them. There was something petulant in choosing to shout over the music, as they were doing.

"Who's your new friend?" said Miranda.

"Nobody. I thought she was an old friend, actually."

"Sure you weren't just attracted to her?"

"No, it was a shock of recognition, of seeing someone

completely familiar. The weird thing is she had the same thing with me, I think." The language available to Doran for describing his cataclysm was cloddish and dead, the words a sequence of corpses laid head to toe.

"Yeah, it's always mutual."

"What's that supposed to mean?"

"Nothing, nothing."

"Look around this party," said Doran. "How many people could you say you've never been in a room together with before? That they didn't actually attend a lower grade in your high school, that you couldn't trace a link to their lives? That's what she and I just did. We're perfect strangers."

"Maybe you saw her on an airplane."

Doran had no answer for this. He fell silent.

Later that night he saw her again, across two rooms, through a doorway. The party had grown. She was talking to someone new, a man, not her friends. He felt he still recognized her, but the sensation hung uselessly in a middle distance, suspended, as in amber, in doubt so thick it was a form of certainty. She irked him, that was all he knew.

• • •

IT WAS two years before he saw the familiar girl again, at another party, again in the hills. They recognized one another immediately.

"I know you," she said, brightening.

"Yes, I know you too, but from where?" The moment he

said it he recalled their conversation. "Of course, how could I forget? You're that girl *I don't know*."

"Oh, yeah." She seemed to grow immensely sad.

They stood together contemplating the privileges of their special relationship, its utter and proven vacancy.

"It's like when you start a book and then you realize you read it before," he said. "You can't really remember anything ahead, only you know each line as it comes to you."

"No surprises to be found, you mean?" She pointed at herself.

"Just a weird kind of pre—" He searched for the word he meant. Pre*formatting*? Pre*cognition*? Pre-*exhaustion*?

"More like a stopped car on the highway slowing down traffic," she said, seemingly uninterested in his ending the unfinished word. "Not a gaudy crash or anything. Just a cop waving you along, saying *Nothing to see here*."

"Doran," he said.

"Vivian."

"I remember. You visiting your friends again?"

"Yup. And before you ask I have no idea whose party this is or what I'm doing here."

"Probably you were looking for me."

"I've got a boyfriend," she said. The line that was always awkward, in anyone's language. Then, before he could respond, she added: "I'm only joking."

"Oh."

"Just didn't want you thinking of me as Ben and Malorie's, oh, sort of *party accessory*. The extra girl, the floater."

"No, never the extra girl. The girl I don't know from anywhere, that's you."

"Funny to meet the girl you don't know, twice," she said. "When there are probably literally thousands of people you do know or anyway could establish a connection with who you never even meet once."

"I'm tempted to say small world."

"Either that or we're very large people."

"But maybe we're evidence of the opposite, I'm thinking now. Large *world*."

"We're not evidence of anything," said Vivian Relf. She shook his hand again. "Enjoy the party."

· · ·

THE NEXT time *was* on an airplane, a coast-to-coast flight. Doran sat in first class. Vivian Relf trundled past him, headed deep into the tail, carry-on hugged to her chest. She didn't spot him.

He mused on sending back champagne with the stewardess, as in a cocktail lounge—*From the man in 3A.* There was probably a really solid reason they didn't allow that. A hundred solid reasons. He didn't dwell on Vivian Relf, watched a movie instead. Barbarian hordes were vanquished in waves of slaughter, twenty thousand feet above the plain.

They spoke at the baggage carousel. She didn't seem overly surprised to see him there.

"As unrelated baggage mysteriously commingles in the

dark belly of an airplane only to be redistributed to its proper possessor in the glare of daylight on the whirring metal belt, so you repeatedly graze my awareness in shunting through the dimmed portals of my life," he said. "Doran Close."

"Vivian Relf," she said, shaking his hand. "But I suspect you knew that."

"Then you've gathered that I'm obsessed with you."

"No, it's that nobody ever forgets my name. It's one of those that sticks in your head."

"Ah."

She stared at him oddly, waiting. He spotted, beneath her sleeve, the unmistakable laminated wristlet of a hospital stay, imprinted RELF, VIVIAN, RM 315.

"I'd propose we share a cab but friends are waiting to pick me up in the white zone." He jerked his thumb at the curb.

"The odds are we're anyway pointed in incompatible directions."

"Ah, if I've learned anything at all in this life it's not to monkey with the odds."

There was a commotion. Some sort of clog at the mouth where baggage was disgorged. An impatient commuter clambered up to straddle the chugging belt. He rolled up suit sleeves and tugged the jammed suitcases out of the chute. The backlog tumbled loose, a miniature avalanche. Doran's suitcase was among those freed. Vivian Relf still waited, peering into the hole as though at a distant horizon. Doran, feeling giddy, left her there.

All that week, between appointments with art collectors and gallerists, he spied for her in the museums and bistros of the vast metropolis, plagued by the ghost of certainty they'd come here, to this far place, this neutral site, *apart but together*, in order to forge some long-delayed truce or compact. The shrouded visages of the locals formed a kind of brick wall, an edifice which met his gaze everywhere: forehead, eyebrows, glasses, grim-drawn lips, cell phones, sandwiches. Against this background she'd have blazed like a sun. But never appeared.

. . .

Oh Vivian Relf! Oh eclipse, oh pale penumbra of my
    yearning!
Pink slip, eviction notice, deleted icon, oh!
Stalked in alleys of my absent noons, there's nobody
knows you better than I!
Translucent voracious Relf-self, I vow here
Never again once to murk you
With pallid tropes of familiarity *or* recognition
You, pure apparition, onion—
Veil of veils only!

. . .

Doran Close, in his capacity as director of acquisitions in drawings and prints, had several times had lunch with

Vander Polymus, the editor of *Wall Art*. He'd heard Polymus mention that he, Polymus, was married. He'd never met the man's wife, though, and it was a surprise, as he stepped across Polymus's threshold for the dinner party, bottle of Cabernet Franc in a scarf of tissue thrust forward in greeting, to discover that the amiable ogre was married to someone he recognized. Not from some previous museum fete or gallery opening but from another life, another frame of reference, years before. Really, from another postulated version of his life, his sense, once, of who he'd be. He knew her despite the boyishly short haircut, the jarring slash of lipstick and bruises of eyeshadow, the freight of silver bracelets: Vander Polymus was married to Vivian Relf.

Meeting her eyes, Doran unconsciously reached up and brushed his fingertips to his shaved skull.

"Doran, Viv," said Polymus, grabbing Doran by the shoulder and tugging him inside. "Throw your coat on the bed. I'll take that. C'mon. Hope you like pernil and bacalao!"

"Hello," she said, and as Doran relinquished the bottle she took his hand to shake.

"Vivian Relf," said Doran.

"Vivian Polymus," she confirmed.

"Shall we pry open your bottle?" said Vander Polymus. "Is it something special? I've got a Rioja I'm itching to sample. You know each other?"

"We met, once," said Vivian. "Other side of the world."

Doran wanted to emend her *once*, but couldn't find his voice.

"Did you fucking fuck my wife?" chortled Polymus, fingers combing his beard. "You'll have to tell me all about it, but save it for dinner. There's people I want you to meet."

So came the accustomed hurdles: the bottles opened and appreciated; the little dinner-party geometries: *No, but of course I know your name* or *If I'm not wrong your gallery represents my dear friend Zeus*; the hard and runny cheeses and the bowl of aggravatingly addictive salted nuts; the dawning apprehension that a single woman in the party of eight had been tipped his way by the scheming Polymus and another couple, who'd brought her along—much as, so long ago, Vivian Relf had been shopped at parties by the couple she'd been visiting. Hurdles? Really these were placed low as croquet wickets. Yet they had to be negotiated for a time, deftly, with a smile, before Doran could at last find himself seated. Beside the single woman, of course, but gratefully, as well, across from Polymus's wife. Vivian Relf.

He raised his glass to her, slightly, wishing to draw her nearer, wishing they could tip their heads together for murmuring.

"I used to think I'd keep running into you forever," he said.

She only smiled. Her husband intruded from the end of the table, his voice commanding. "What is it with you two?" Irrationally, Polymus's own impatience seemed to encompass the years since Doran and Vivian's first meeting, the otherwise forgettable, and forgotten, party. Doran wondered if anyone else on the planet had reason to recall that vanished archipelago of fume, conversation, and disco, tonight or ever. The ancient party was like a radio signal dopplering through outer space, it seemed to him now.

"You fuck him, Viv?" said Polymus. "Inquiring minds want to know."

"No," said Vivian Relf-Polymus. "No, but we were probably flirting. This was a long time ago."

Polymus and his wife had captured the attention of the whole table, with evident mutual pleasure.

"We had this funny thing," Doran felt compelled to explain. "You remember? We didn't know anyone in common. You seemed really familiar, but we'd never met before."

This drew a handful of polite laughs, cued principally by the word *funny*, and perhaps by Doran's jocular tone. Beneath it he felt desperate. Vander Polymus only scowled, as for comic effect he might scowl at an awkwardly hung painting, or at a critical notice with which he violently disagreed.

"What I remember is you had these awful friends," said Vivian. "They didn't hesitate to show they found me a poor way for you to be spending your time. What was that tall moody boy's name?"

"Top," said Doran, only remembering as he blurted it.

He hadn't thought of Top for years, had in fact forgotten
Top was present at the Vivian Relf Party.

"Were you breaking up with some girl that night?"

"No," said Doran. "Nothing like that." He couldn't remember.

"If looks could kill."

Those people mean nothing to me, Doran wished to
cry. *They barely did at the time. And now, what was it,
ten years later?* It was Vivian Relf who mattered, couldn't
she see?

"Do you remember the airport?" he asked.

"Ah, the *airport*," said Polymus, with a connoisseur's
sarcasm. "Now we're getting somewhere. Tell us about the
airport."

The table chuckled nervously, all in deference to their
host.

"I haven't the faintest idea what he's talking about, my
love."

"It's nothing," said Doran. "I saw you, ah, at an airport
once." He suddenly wished to diminish it, in present company. He saw now that something precious was being
taken from him in full view, a treasure he'd found in his
possession only at the instant it was squandered. *I wrote a
poem to you once, Vivian Relf*, he said silently, behind a
sip of excellent Rioja. Doran knew it was finer, much more
interesting, than the wine he'd brought, the Cabernet
Franc they'd sipped with their appetizers.

He might have known Vivian Relf better than anyone he
actually knew, Doran thought now. Or anyway, he'd

wanted to. It ought to mean the same thing. His soul creaked in irrelevant despair.

"This is boring," pronounced Vander Polymus.

The dinner party rose up and swallowed them, as it was meant to.

Planet Big Zero

MY HOUSE IS PROTECTED FROM THE STREET by a wooden fence six feet high, so solidly built that it's practically a wall. You can't look through it. The fence gate swings open smoothly, an inch from the paved walkway, without sticking or wobbling. Returning home a few days ago, I stepped up and pushed the gate open, as I always do, without breaking my stride. This day the gate bumped hard against something on the other side.

Annoyed, I pushed harder, and stepped through the space I'd wedged open. Lying on the walkway, rubbing his head, was a bum. I'd whacked him on the top of his skull with the gate. After a confused moment I grasped the situation: he'd ducked in from the street, then stretched out to warm in the sun in the first place he found. I live next door to a supermarket. He was probably napping after a meal of salvage from the dumpster in the alley. I knew that bums sometimes slept the night in the alley, though they always kept out of sight.

He wasn't knocked out. He made a sort of rasping, moaning sound and rolled onto his side.

Then we had the strangest conversation.

"You okay?" I said, defensively gruff.

"Yeah," he said. He was bald on top, so I could see that there wasn't a gash.

"That's a hell of a place to be," I said, justifying myself.

He said something I couldn't quite make out. It sounded like, "Every place has its price."

"What?"

"That's the price of this place." Or something. I was already walking away, toward my door. I'd seen that he was both unharmed and harmless.

"Well, take care of yourself," I said.

"Don't worry about me," he said.

Then I went inside, and for the briefest moment, tried to think about what had happened. *I just hit a man in the head with a big piece of wood*, I told myself. A part of me insisted that it was a notable event, something disturbing, something extreme. I'd certainly never done anything like it before.

But that part of me lost out. My attention just slid away. I literally *couldn't* keep my mind on it.

I mention this because of the light it sheds on what happened with Matthew.

· · ·

WHEN MATTHEW and I were in high school we had a running joke that I think epitomized our sense of humor. Our school featured special programs for musically talented students. For that reason, or for no reason at all, there was a bust of Toscanini in the middle of the main hall of the building. It was a dingy bronze, slightly larger than life-size. Toscanini gazed out with a stolid, heroic air, his thick oxidized hair flowing back in the sculptor's imaginary breeze. He could have been a general, or a football coach, but a plaque on the pillar informed us that it was in fact Toscanini. It was typical of Matthew and me that we even noticed the sculpture. I doubt if any of the other students could have confirmed its existence if we'd mentioned it to them. We never did.

The joke was exclusively between us and some unseen janitor or security guard. Every week or so for a whole term, on our way out of the building after our last class, Matthew and I would hurriedly tape a pair of eyeglass frames, crudely fashioned from torn notebook paper and scotch tape, across Toscanini's glaring eyes. The glasses were never there when we returned in the morning. They were probably torn away within minutes, but that didn't matter to us. The sight of the paper glasses on the bronze was funny, but only initially was it the point of the joke.

The real point was saying it, again and again. "Toscanini's glasses." As though those glasses were a landmark, the one certainty in an uncertain universe. Whatever subject was at hand, the glasses were the comparison we'd reach for first. "What didn't you understand? It was as clear as Toscanini's glasses." Or "Cool, man, like Toscanini's glasses." Or "No more urgent than, say, Toscanini's glasses." If one of us forgot what he was going to say, the other would gently suggest, "Something about Toscanini's glasses?"

It was a joke about futility, and at the same time a joke about will, and subjectivity. If we filibustered the glasses into existence between us did it matter that the paper-and-tape glasses didn't persist? Worlds seemed to hang in the balance of that unspoken question, and in a way they did. Our worlds. The glasses stood for our own paper-thin new sensibilities, thrust against the bronze of the adult world. Were we viable? Did we have to convince others, or was it enough just to convince ourselves?

The question was made immediate by our careers as students. Did it matter that you were smarter than your English teacher if she could fail you for cutting class to smoke pot in the park? Matthew and I gave her that chance, and she took it. When college-application time rolled around, the costs were suddenly apparent. You couldn't get into an Ivy League school on the strength of private jokes.

Actually, I did. For the essay section of my Yale application I drew a ten-page comic, of the soul-searching,

R. Crumb variety. It took me three weeks, and it was by far the most sustained effort I'd made in the four years of high school, or in my life to that point. I remember Matthew calling me at home during those weeks, wanting to know what was wrong. I couldn't explain.

The comic led to an unusual interview with a Yale scout. The first question he asked was what my favorite single book was. I said *Travels in Arabia Deserta*, which I'd never read. He looked taken aback. "That's *my* favorite book," he said. "I didn't realize anyone your age was reading it." "Yeah, well," I said. "I'm an autodidact." I hoped that would account for my grades. I don't know if it did, but I had the scout eating out of my hand after the lucky coincidence. Fortunately he didn't ask me what I liked about *Arabia Deserta*.

Matthew got into Reed. I helped him get the application out, in one desperate night before the deadline. Reed is one of those colleges where they don't give grades, where you can major in things like harmonica or earth sculpture. It's in the Pacific Northwest, far from New York, which probably would have been good for him. But he didn't go. He convinced his parents that he needed a year abroad before he could decide what to do. Sending him to college would have cost about the same, so they went for it. He and his marijuana fumes were out of the house either way.

Matthew was talking about becoming a Zen monk a lot at that time, and he even carried around an Alan Watts book called *The Wisdom of Insecurity* for a while. I'm sure he thought our pranks were a form of native Zen. An example: We took an 8-by-11 sheet of clear Mylar to the Xerox shop and asked for a copy. The clerk indulged us. The result was a photograph of the inside of the machine, of course, but Matthew insisted on calling it "a copy of nothing." Just like one hand clapping, see? He cared nothing about Buddhism, needless to say. If there had been such a thing as a Dada monk he would have wanted to become that. But Zen it was, so he went to Asia.

Matthew visited me once at Yale, junior year. I lived in a suite with a roommate, and I was embarrassed to have Matthew stay there. He and I were beginning to look different. He was sunburned and wiry and seemed quite a bit older. He was still dressed like a boy but he looked like a man. At Yale we all dressed like men but looked like boys, except for a few who were working on beer stomachs.

Matthew was back temporarily from Thailand, where, he explained excitedly, he'd gotten involved with a charismatic drug lord named Khan Shah. Khan Shah was more powerful than the government, Matthew said, and was trying to legitimize his rule by making poppy cultivation legal. He was a man of the people. Matthew was learning to speak Thai so he could translate Khan Shah's manifestos.

This didn't sound like Zen to me, and I told Matthew so. He laughed.

"Are you doing what you want to do?" he asked me suddenly.

That question didn't compute for me at the time.

Matthew was making me very, very nervous. I could still admire him, but I didn't want him in my life.

Cracking old jokes for cover, I hustled him back down to New York with excuses about a girlfriend's demands and a paper I had to write. He spent just one night.

That was the last I saw of him for eight years. Except for postcards. Here's one from a few years back. The front shows Elton John, in spangled glasses. In Matthew's hand on the back it says "Vacant Lot/Living Chemist." No return address. The postmark is Santa Fe, New Mexico.

•   •   •

I ONLY had an hour's warning. He got my number from information, he explained on the phone. I gave him the address. An hour later he knocked on my door.

He wobbled slightly. "I parked in the green zone," he said.

"That's fine, it's two hours." I stared. He was still tall and bony, but his face was fleshy and red. I immediately wondered if I looked as bad, if I'd lost as much.

"Here," he said. "I brought you this."

It was a rock, fist-sized, gray with veins of white. I took it.

"Thanks," I said, checking the irony in my voice. I didn't know whether I was supposed to think it was mainly funny or mainly profound that he'd brought me a rock.

If it was high school there would have been a punch

line. He would have led me out to the curb to see the trunk-load of identical rocks in his car.

Ten years later, that kind of follow-through was gone. Matthew's gestures were shrouded and gnomic. Trees falling in forests.

"Come in," I said.

"I saw the Piggly Wiggly when I parked," he said. "I thought I'd get some beer."

It was two in the afternoon. "Okay," I said.

A few minutes later he was back in the doorway with a rustling paper bag. He unloaded a six-pack of Sierra Nevada into my fridge and opened a tall aluminum canister of Japanese beer to drink right away. We poured it into two glasses. I wrote off getting anything accomplished that afternoon.

He leaned back and smiled at me, but his eyes were nervous. "Nice place," he said.

"It's a place where I can get work done," I said, feeling weirdly defensive.

"I see your stuff whenever I can," he said earnestly. "My parents clip them for me."

I draw a one-page comic called *Planet Big Zero*, for a free music magazine produced by a record-store chain. Once a month my characters, Dr. Fahrenheit and Sniveling Toon (and their little dog, Louie Louie), have a stupid adventure and review a new CD by a major rock act.

Somewhere in there you might detect the dying heartbeat of Toscanini's glasses. It's a living, anyway. Better than a living recently, since a cable video channel bought rights to develop *Planet* into a weekly animated feature, and hired me to do scripts and storyboards.

"I didn't realize your folks were into rock journalism," I said.

"My parents are really proud of you," Matthew said, working diligently on his beer. He wasn't being sarcastic. There was nothing challenging left in his persona, except what I projected.

He told me his story. Since Santa Fe he'd been in Peru, taking pictures of plinths and other ancient structures. He talked a lot about "sites." The term covered a sculpture in Texas made of upended Cadillacs half buried in the desert, stone rings in Tibet, a circular graveyard in Paris, and Wall Street skyscrapers. He'd shot hundreds of rolls of film. None of it was developed. He was trying to get funding to create a CD-ROM. In the tales he told there were ghosts, mostly women, scurrying out of the frame. An expatriate Englishwoman he'd lived with in Mexico City who'd thrown him out. A female journalist who'd been his collaborator, then disappeared with his only photos of an Inca burial site that had since been destroyed. And the bitch in the Florida Keys just now who'd stolen his camera after a shared three-day drunk.

I live in Connecticut, an hour out of the city if there's no traffic. Matthew had driven up to see me in his parents' car. He was in New York trying to convince his parents to cash out ten thousand dollars in zero coupon bonds they were holding in his name, presumably for when he married and bought a house. He was willing to take a hit on early-withdrawal penalties, so that he could use what remained to fund his return to Peru.

He'd become some combination of an artist with the temperament, but no art, and Thor Heyerdahl without a raft.

The Japanese canister was empty. Matthew went into the kitchen for the first of the Sierras, unapologetically. He wasn't drinking like he was on a tear, or wanted to be. It was as though the beer was a practical necessity, like he needed it for ballast.

"If you don't want to drive back down tonight you can stay in the garage," I told him. "It's set up as a guest room. You can pee in the sink in there. I'll give you a key to the house so you can shower or whatever."

"That's great," he said. His look was humble and piercing, both. "You know, it's really amazing to see you again."

I sort of flinched. "The same," I said.

"It's amazing how little has changed after all this time."

I wasn't aware of that being the case, in any sense at all. But I nodded.

That night we got on a roll in safe territory, talking about high school. The Water Fountain Trick. The Literary Excuse Me. Mother Communication Hates You. Falling Down Jesus Park. Toscanini's Glasses. Then, fueled by beer, I told him a bit about my life, my short marriage, the novel I couldn't sell, the years of legal proofreading. Matthew drank and listened. He listened well.

Then he started telling me about his idea for a screen-play we were going to write together. "Has there ever been a thriller set in Antarctica?" he asked, eyes burning.

"*Ice Station Zebra*," I said. "Rock Hudson's in it. It's really bad. Listen, I'm bushed."

He slept in. I was working at my desk for hours before I heard him go in through the kitchen, up to the bathroom for a shower. The water ran for almost twenty minutes. I'm not sure, but I think he must have come out while I was on the phone with my Hollywood agent.

As I get older I find that the friendships that are the most certain, ultimately, are the ones where you and the other person have made substantial amounts of money for one another. Those histories have a breadth, an unspoken ease, that others, even siblings or ex-wives, just can't match. My Hollywood agent is about my age, and when I talk to him I feel he knows who I am, because he helped make me who I am. We're a conspiracy, and a much more reliable one than most.

Some time after I'd hung up the phone, I became aware of Matthew standing in the doorway of my office. "Did you hear me talking to you?" he said.

"Uh, no."

His eyes were ringed and dark. He didn't speak.

"There's coffee in the kitchen," I said. "It's still hot."

When he returned with the coffee he came all the way into the room and stood in front of me. He seemed dis-concerted.

"I think I'll go check out that old foundry today," he

said. "There's some wrecked equipment I always wanted to take pictures of."

"No camera," I reminded him.

"Well, I guess I'll just go look at it."

Ruins, I thought. Wrecks, shambles, margins. Zen junk.

"That's fine, I'll be here," I said. "I have some stuff to do. We can go out for dinner tonight."

"We could cook something," he began. I could see him grasping, trying to frame some larger question.

"I'd like to take you out," I said—magnanimity being one of the most effective ways of ending conversations. I was thinking of my work. I had to get back to harnessing our high-school sensibility to the task of selling compact discs.

. . .

HE WAS back at five, with another bag from the Piggly Wiggly. Inside was a full six-pack, and another one full of empties. He'd been out all day looking at sites and drinking beer from a paper bag. He put the empties on the porch and the six in the fridge, like an obedient dog moving slippers to the bedroom.

I'd arranged for us to meet a couple of friends for dinner. A science-fiction writer who does scenarios for interactive video games, and a screenwriter. We all have the same Hollywood agent, which is how we met. I figured the screenwriter could sober Matthew up about his script ideas. I didn't want to eat dinner with Matthew alone anyway.

We met for drinks first. By the time we got to the restaurant Matthew was lagging behind, already so invisible that the maître d' said, "Table for three?"

He barely spoke during dinner. At the end of the night we parted at my driveway, me to my front door, Matthew to the garage.

"Well, good night," I said.

He stopped. "You know, I realize I don't have everything quite together," he said.

"You've got a lot of interesting projects going," I said.

"I'm not asking you for anything." He glared, just briefly.

"Of course not."

"I feel strange around you," he said. "I can't explain." He looked at his hands, held them up against the light of the moon.

"You're just getting used to the way I am now," I said. "I've changed."

"No, it's me," he said.

"Get some sleep," I said.

I didn't see him in the morning, just heard the shower running, and the door to the refrigerator opening and closing.

.   .   .

ABOUT A week later, I hit on the idea of putting Matthew into *Planet Big Zero* as a character. It was a way of assuaging my own guilt, and of compartmentalizing the experience of seeing him again. I guess I also wanted to establish the connection between our old wide-open, searching form of humor and my current smug, essentially closed form.

As I drew Matthew into the panels it occurred to me that I was casting him into a prison by publishing him in the cartoon. Then I realized how silly that was. If he was in a prison he was there already, and the cartoon had nothing to do with it. He'd be delighted to see himself. I imagined showing it to him. Then I realized I wouldn't. Anyway, I finished the cartoon, and FedExed it to my editor.

Who hated it. "What's that guy doing there?" he said on the phone.

"He's a new character," I said.

"He's not funny," said the editor. "Can you take him out?"

"You want me to take him out?"

"He's not intrinsic to any of the scenes," said my editor. "He's just standing around."

.   .   .

THAT WAS two months ago. The point is, it wasn't until just the other day, when I hit the sleeping bum on the head with the gate, that I really gave any thought to the way things turned out. So much of what we do is automatic, so much of life becomes invisible. For instance, I've been buying six-packs and putting them in the fridge, but it isn't me drinking them. The empties pile up on the porch. I always forget to bring them out to the curb on recycling day. Sometimes the bums prowl around for bottles and do my work for me. I think somebody somewhere gives them a nickel apiece for them—another invisible operation, among so many.

Matthew's parents' car got towed after two weeks. It must have had ten or fifteen tickets pinned under the wiper. The authorities are pretty vigilant about that around here. As for Matthew, he's still in the garage. But he's been rendered completely transparent, unless, I suppose, you happen to be wearing Toscanini's glasses.

The Glasses

Rows of frames sat on glass shelves, clear lenses reflecting gray light from the Brooklyn avenue. Outside, rain fell. At the door a cardboard box waited for umbrellas. The carpet was pink and yellow, to the limits of the floor, to the tightly seamed glass cases. The empty shop was like a cartoonist's eyeball workshop, hundreds of bare outlines yearning for pupils, for voices. They fell short of expression themselves. The whole shop fell short. There was no radio. The white-coated opticians leaned on their glass counters, dreaming of their wives, of beautiful women who needed glasses. One of them moved into the rear of the shop and made a call.

The other turned as the door chimed, two notes blurred momentarily in the rain's hiss.

"You're back."

"Damn fucking right I'm back." The black man wiped his feet just inside the door, though there wasn't a mat, then jogged forward into the shop. He wore a baseball cap, and his glasses.

The optician didn't move. "You don't need to use language," he said.

They'd sold him his glasses yesterday. One hundred dollars. He'd paid with cash, not out of a wallet.

The customer bounced from one foot to the other like a boxer. An ingrown beard scarred the underside of his long jaw. He pushed his chin forward, keeping his hands by his side. "Look. Same damn thing."

The optician grunted slightly and moved to look. He was as tall as the customer, and fatter. "A smudge," he said.

He was still purring in his boredom. This distraction hadn't persuaded him yet that it would become an event, a real dent in the afternoon.

"*Scratched*," said the customer. "Same as the last pair. If you can't fix the problem why'd you sell me the damn glasses?"

"A smudge," said the optician. "Clean it off. Here."

The customer ducked backward. "Keep off. Don't fool with me. Can't clean it off. They're already messed up. Like the old ones. They're *all messed up*."

"Let me see," said the optician.

"Where's Dr. Bucket? I want to talk to the doctor."

"*Burkhardt.* And he's not a doctor. Let me see." The optician drew in his stomach, adjusted his own glasses.

"*You're* not the doctor, man." The customer danced away recklessly, still thrusting out his chin.

"We're both the same," said the optician wearily. "We make glasses. Let me see."

The second optician came out of the back, smoothed his hair, and said, "What?"

"Bucket!"

The second optician looked at the first, then turned to the customer. "Something wrong with the glasses?"

"Same thing as yesterday. Same place. Look." Checking his agitation, he stripped his glasses off with his right hand and offered them to the second optician.

"First of all, you should take them off with two hands, like I showed you," said the second optician. He pinched the glasses at the two hinges, demonstrating. Then he turned them and raised them to his own face.

The inside of the lenses were marked, low and close to the nose.

"You touched them. That's the problem."

"No."

"Of course you did. That's fingerprints."

"Damn, Bucket, man. I'll show you the old ones. You can't even fix the problem."

"The problem is you touched them. Here." The second

optician went to the counter and dipped the glasses in a shallow bath of cleanser, dried them with a chamois cloth. The customer bobbed forward anxiously, trying to see.

"What do you, scratch at your eyes all the time?" said the first optician, smiling now. The problem was solved.

"Shut up," said the customer, pointing a finger at the first optician. "Just shut up. You're not my doctor on this."

"Nobody is," said the first optician. "You don't need a doctor, you need to keep your hands out of your eyes."

"Shut up."

The second optician glared at the first. He handed the glasses to the customer. "Let me see you put them on."

The customer bent his head down and lifted the glasses to his face.

"Wait a minute, I couldn't see . . ."

"It's the *fit*."

"The bill of your cap was in the way," said the first optician.

"Put them on again," said the second.

"Same thing," said the customer, shaking his head. He pulled off the glasses, again with one hand. "Look. Still there. Little scratches."

The first optician stepped up close to the customer. "Sure. You touched it again. When I couldn't see. It's how you put them on."

"He uses his thumbs," said the second, snorting.

"Little scratches, man. I paid a hundred dollars. Second day I got these little scratches again. Might as well kept the old ones." He thrust the glasses at the first optician.

"They're not scratched," said the first optician. "Just dirty. Your hands are dirty."

The customer flared his nostrils, twitched his cheek, raised his eyebrows. "That's *weak*, Bucket. I come in here show you a pair of glasses get all rubbed and scratched, I'm looking for some *help*. You tell me I need some new glasses. Now the new ones got the *same* problem, you tell me I got dirty *hands*. These the glasses you sold me, my man."

The second optician let air slip very slowly through his tightened lips. "Your old pair was scratched. You had them, what, ten years? They were falling off your face. The hinges were shot, the nosepiece was gone. The lens touched your cheek." He paused to let this litany sink in. "The glasses I sold you are fine. The fit is fine. You just have to break some habits."

"Habits!"

"He's a clown," said the first optician, leaning back against the counter, sticking out his belly. "We should've thrown him out yesterday."

"Instead you took my *money*," hissed the customer. "Good enough for you yesterday. You couldn't see *black* for all the green yesterday. Now I look black to you. Now I'm a clown."

"You think we need your hundred dollars?" The first optician managed a laugh.

"That's not necessary," said the second, to the customer. He ignored his partner. "We'll take care of you. Sit down, let me look at the fit."

"Shit. Your man needs to shut up."

"Okay, please." The second optician pulled up a chair from beside the counter. The padding was pink to match the carpet.

"Sit down."

The partners fell easily into a good optician/bad optician routine. It was pure instinct. Perhaps the customer sensed his options dwindling, perhaps not. Probably he did. The air went out of him a little as he took the chair.

And the glasses, the proof, were in enemy hands. The second optician was rinsing them again.

"Shit, Bucket," said the customer, petulance in his voice now. "What you know about my *habits*?"

"Okay," said the second optician, ignoring the remark. His voice was soothing. "I just want to see you put them on. Just naturally, like you would. Don't push them into your face. They won't fall off. Just drop them over your ears. Then I'll check the fit."

He offered the glasses, then pulled them back as the customer reached for them. "Take off your hat," he said admonishingly.

The customer took off his hat. His hair was grooved where the lip of the hat had rested. The first optician, watching from his place at the counter, reflexively reached up and fluffed his own hair.

"Here you go. Nice and easy." The second optician handed over the glasses.

The customer stuffed the hat in his ass pocket, then raised the glasses with both hands, holding them by the earpieces awkwardly. His hands trembled.

"That's it," said the second optician. "Let's have a look at the fit."

The customer dropped his hands to his lap. The second optician brought his face close to the customer's. For a moment they were still, breathing together tightly, eyes flickering. The intimacy calmed the customer. He was in some sense now getting his due, his money's worth. He could feel the second optician's breath graze his cheek.

Then the second optician saw the marks.

"Wait a minute," said the second optician, straightening his body. "They're still smudged."

"I told you!" said the customer.

"He touched them again," said the first optician, back at the counter. "I told you, he puts his thumb on the lens."

"You touched them again," said the second optician.

"You watched me! You saw! I didn't touch them!"

The second optician shook his head, crestfallen. "I don't understand how it happened."

"Simple, he touched them," said the first.

"Liar!" shouted the customer. "You watched me."

"Listen," said the second optician, rallying, a little frenzied. "This doesn't make sense. What do you think? They smudged themselves? You touched them!"

"I want my money back, Bucket."

"Look, I can give you your money back, it's not going to do any good. You're screwing up your glasses yourself. It's going to be the same wherever you go."

"It's the fit."

"What are you saying, fit?" interrupted the first optician.

"You think they're touching your cheek?"

"That's right. My cheek."

"Show me where," said the first, leaning in.

"For chrissake, don't make him put his hands up there," said the second. The opticians had traded places now, the fierce, the patient. Only the customer was unperturbed, true to himself. He moved his hand with slow drama, like a magician, to point at his face. Shifting and sighing, the opticians closed around him to see.

The rain outside slowed, died. Cars whirred through the water in the street.

"It's my *cheek*," reminded the customer.

"Maybe your last ones touched you there," said the second optician. "Your nosepiece was all worn down. These don't touch."

"I feel it."

"No, you don't. You're used to touching yourself there, putting your fingers in there," said the second. "That's what I meant by habits."

"You don't know," said the customer quietly, with a Buddhist calm. "Now you got to give me my money back."

"We'll see about that," said the second optician grimly. He plucked the glasses from the customer's face.

"This is getting silly," said the first optician to the second. "Give him his money. Get him out of here."

"I'll make him sit here all night if I have to," said the second. "He's putting his fingers on them."

"I got all the time in the world," said the customer happily.

"Sit still," said the second optician. He again dried the glasses with the chamois, and replaced them on the customer's face. "Keep your hands down."

The customer sat, his hands on his knees, the chord of tension in his body stilled at some cost. The second optician leaned in close to the customer's face to inspect the juncture of nosepiece and nose.

"How long are we going to keep him here?" said the first optician pleadingly.

"I told you, as long as it takes."

"You're kidding me."

"Help me watch him. Watch his hands."

The customer smiled, delighted now. He could play this game and win. They'd see the scratches reappear. He focused on his hands. They were all focused on his hands. He kept his hands on his knees.

"We gotta get him out of the way at least," said the first optician.

"Behind the counter," said the second. In his determination he had an answer for everything.

"Here you go, Bucket," said the customer.

"Keep your hands down!" said the second optician. "Let me move the chair. Joe, watch his hands."

The customer was installed behind the counter, hands on his knees, chin up, waiting. The bill of his cap jutted from his back pocket.

The opticians leaned against the wall and the counter,

inspecting the customer as though he were a horse on which they'd bet, and they gamblers looking for some giveaway imperfections, some tremble in its flank.

"He's gonna touch them," said the first optician.

"He *wants* to," said the second. "But he knows we're watching."

"You'll see," said the customer.

"Look at his hands," said the first. "He can't take it, he's gotta go up there. It's like a tic, a whatchamacallit. He's got like Tourette's syndrome or something."

"Fuck you, motherfucker," said the customer genially.

"We've got forever," said the second optician, his tone smooth, his calm restored. "We'll wait it out."

The door chimed. They all turned. The new customer was young, in his late twenties. A boy to these men, a boy in a sweater. He turned to the glass shelves on the wall.

"Can I help you find something?" said the second optician, stepping up. Then he turned and hissed: "Watch his hands!"

"Just browsing," said the new customer, and immediately wondered: Was browsing the right word for glasses?

And: Who was that black man in the chair?

"You have glasses before?" asked the second optician.

"Yes, uh, I don't always wear them."

"You want to see anything, let me know."

"Okay."

The new customer moved along the wall of frames, searching for the expensive ones, the Japanese titanium-alloy designs.

Almost involuntarily, he glanced back, and the black man in the chair bugged his eyes at him. A plea for help?

The two opticians in their white coats, gold glasses, and puffy hair reminded him of Nazis. Nazi doctors. Or perhaps Mafia. Yes, definitely Mafia. He'd heard about this neighborhood. He knew of the dark old economic engines still humming away under the bright yuppie surface.

But should he get involved?

He slid closer along the back wall and had another look. The black man sat with his hands on his knees, obviously containing himself. His keepers' eyes shifted from their prisoner to the new customer, watching. What was it they'd said—*Watch his hands?*

"Are you okay?" the new customer blurted.

"Fuck you think, jackass? Fuck you staring at? You see something wrong with me?"

The black man gesticulated, waving the new customer away, and the second optician said: "The hands, the hands."

"What's wrong with his hands?" said the new customer, even as he backed away.

"Mind your own business," said the first optician.

"Damn. He thinks I'm a shoplifter, Bucket. Fucking racist motherfucker."

"I'm sorry."

"Tell him, Bucket. I'm a paying customer."

"It's okay," said the new customer, moving to the door, and out, into the dying afternoon. The sun had arrived just to depart, to throw a few long shadows around as though it had worked the whole day.

The three of them watched the new customer disappear from view of the shop window.

"Now you're scaring off our customers," said the second optician fondly.

"Screw him," said the first optician, waving dismissively at the door. "He was a looker. Just browsing, you heard him."

"Racist jackass got to go jumping to conclusions," said the customer, fingers bouncing on his knees.

"Let me see your hands," said the first optician.

"You got eyes!"

"No, I mean turn them over. Let me take a look."

The customer furrowed his brow. The first optician took the customer's left hand in his own and gently turned it over.

"You're got very rough hands," said the first optician. "Look at your fingertips. Very rough."

The second optician bent in to look, and so did the customer, their heads all drawing together.

"See that?" said the first optician. "Think he could of scratched up his lenses with his fingers like that?"

"Hmmm," said the second optician. "Plastic lenses, sure. Like his old ones. Not glass. Only smudge glass."

"*If* I touched it," said the customer.

"Yeah, right, *if*," said the first optician, still holding the customer's hand. "We're suspending judgment."

"That's what makes you a good man," said the customer. "You want to do the right thing."

"Yes we do," said the first optician. "That's why we're sitting here. Long as it takes."

"Don't want to go jumping to no conclusions."

"Never."

"Damn straight."

The first optician went to the counter and took out a pack of cigarettes. The second optician sighed.

"You got a good man here, Bucket," said the customer, pointing. "I spoke too soon."

"Watch your hands," said the second optician.

"You'll watch 'em for me, Bucket. I know you will."

The sun was down. Shops outside rolled down their gates. Restaurant deliverymen on green bicycles began to fill the street. Men dragged home milk and flowers and shuttered umbrellas.

The first optician lit another cigarette and put it in the customer's mouth for him, so the customer could keep his hands on his knees.

The second optician moved into the back of the shop, to call his wife, to say he'd be late.

The Dystopianist, Thinking of His Rival, Is Interrupted by a Knock on the Door

THE DYSTOPIANIST DESTROYED THE WORLD again that morning, before making any phone calls or checking his mail, before even breakfast. He destroyed it by cabbages. The Dystopianist's scribbling fingers pushed notes onto the page: a protagonist, someone, *a tousle-haired, well-intentioned geneticist*, had designed a new kind of cabbage for use as a safety device—*the "air bag cabbage."* The air bag cabbage mimicked those decorative cabbages planted by the sides of roads to spell names of towns, or arranged by color—red, white, and that eerie, iridescent cabbage indigo—to create American flags. It looked like any other cabbage. But underground was a network of gas-bag roots, *vast inflatable roots*, filled with pressurized air. So, *at the slightest tap*, no, more than a tap, or vandals would set them off for fun, right, *given a serious blow such as only a car traveling at thirty miles or more per hour could deliver*, the heads of the air bag cabbages would instantly inflate, drawing air from the root system, to cushion the impact of the crash, saving lives, *preventing costly property loss*. Only—

The Dystopianist pushed away from his desk, and squinted through the blinds at the sun-splashed street below. School buses lined his block every morning, like vast tipped orange-juice cartons spilling out the human vitamin of youthful lunacy, that chaos of jeering voices and dancing tangled shadows in the long morning light. The Dystopianist was hungry for breakfast. He didn't know yet how the misguided safety cabbages fucked up the world. He couldn't say what *grievous chain of circumstances* led from the *innocuous genetic novelty* to another *crushing totalitarian regime*. He didn't know what light the cabbages shed on the *death urge in human societies*. He'd work it out, though. That was his job. First Monday of each month the Dystopianist came up with his idea, the *green poison fog* or *dehumanizing fractal download* or *alienating architectural fad* which would open the way to another ruined or oppressed reality. Tuesday he began making his extrapolations, and he had the rest of the month to get it right. Today was Monday, so the cabbages were enough.

The Dystopianist moved into the kitchen, poured a second cup of coffee, and pushed slices of bread into the toaster. The *Times* Metro section headline spoke of the capture of a celebrated villain, an addict and killer who'd crushed a pedestrian's skull with a cobblestone. The Dystopianist read his paper while scraping his toast with shreds of ginger marmalade, knife rushing a little surf of butter ahead of the crystalline goo. He read intently to the end of the account, taking pleasure in the story.

The Dystopianist hated bullies. He tried to picture himself standing behind darkened glass, fingering perps in a line-up, couldn't. He tried to picture himself standing in the glare, head flinched in arrogant dejection, waiting to be fingered, but this was even more impossible. He stared at the photo of the apprehended man and unexpectedly the Dystopianist found himself thinking vengefully, hatefully, of his rival.

Once the Dystopianist had had the entire dystopian field to himself. There was just him and the Utopianists. The Dystopianist loved reading the Utopianists' stories, their dim, hopeful scenarios, which were published in magazines like *Expectant* and *Encouraging*. The Dystopianist routinely purchased them newly minted from the newsstands and perverted them the very next day in his own work, plundering the Utopianists' motifs for dark inspiration. Even the garishly sunny illustrated covers of the magazines were fuel. The Dystopianist stripped them from the magazines' spines and pinned them up over his desk, then raised his pen like Death's sickle and plunged those dreamily ineffectual worlds into ruin.

The Utopianists were older men who'd come into the field from the sciences or from academia: Professor this or that, like Dutch burghers from a cigar box. The Dystopianist had appeared in print like a rat among them, a burrowing animal laying turds on their never-to-be-realized blueprints. He liked his role. Every once in a blue moon the Dystopianist agreed to appear in public alongside the Utopianists, on a panel at a university or a conference. They loved to gather, *the fools*, in fluorescent-lit halls behind tables decorated with sweating pitchers of ice water. They were always eager to praise him in public by calling him one of their own. The Dystopianist ignored them, refusing even the water from their pitchers. He played directly to the audience members who'd come to see him, who shared his low opinion of the Utopianists. The Dystopianist could always spot his readers by their black trench coats, their acne, their greasily teased hair, their earphones, resting around their collars, trailing to Walkmans secreted in coat pockets.

The Dystopianist's rival was a Utopianist, but he wasn't like the others.

The Dystopianist had known his rival, the man he privately called *the Dire One*, since they were children like those streaming into the schoolyard below. *Eeny meeny miney moe!* they'd chanted together, each trembling in fear of being permanently *"It,"* of never casting off their permanent case of *cooties*. They weren't quite friends, but the Dystopianist and the Dire One had been bullied together by the older boys, quarantined in their shared nerdishness, forced to pool their resentments. In glum resignation they'd swapped Wacky Packages stickers and algebra homework answers, offered sticks of Juicy Fruit and squares of Now-N-Later, forging a loser's deal of consolation.

Then they were separated after junior high school, and the Dystopianist forgot his uneasy schoolmate.

It was nearly a year now since the Dire Utopianist had first arrived in print. The Dystopianist had trundled home with the latest issue of *Heartening*, expecting the usual laughs, and been blindsided instead by the Dire Utopianist's first story. The Dystopianist didn't recognize his rival by name, but he knew him for a rival instantly.

The Dire Utopianist's trick was to write in a style which was *nominally* utopian. His fantasies were nearly as credible as everyday experience, but bathed in a radiance of glory. They glowed with wishfulness. The other Utopianists' stories were crude candy floss by comparison. The Dire Utopianist's stories weren't blunt or ideological. He'd invented an *aesthetics* of utopia.

Fair enough. If he'd stopped at this burnished, closely observed dream of human life, the Dire Utopianist would be no threat. Sure, heck, let there be one genius among the Utopianists, all the better. It raised the bar. The Dystopianist took the Dire One's mimetic brilliance as a spur of inspiration: Look closer! Make it real!

But the Dire Utopianist didn't play fair. He didn't stop at utopianism, no. He poached on the Dystopianist's turf, he encroached. By limning a world so subtly transformed, so barely *nudged* into the ideal, the Dire One's fictions cast a shadow back onto the everyday. They induced a despair of inadequacy in the real. Turning the last page of one of the Dire Utopianist's stories, the reader felt a mortal pang at slipping back into his own daily life, which had been proved morbid, crushed, unfair.

This was the Dire One's pitiless art: *his utopias wrote reality itself into the most persuasive dystopia imaginable.* At the Dystopianist's weak moments he knew his stories were by comparison contrived and crotchety, their darkness forced.

It was six weeks ago that *Vivifying* had published the Dire One's photograph, and the Dystopianist had recognized his childhood acquaintance.

The Dire Utopianist never appeared in public. There was no clamor for him to appear. In fact, he wasn't even particularly esteemed among the Utopianists, an irony which rankled the Dystopianist. It was as though the Dire One didn't mind seeing his work buried in the insipid utopian magazines. He didn't seem to crave recognition of any kind, let alone the hard-won oppositional stance the Dystopianist treasured. It was almost as though the Dire One's stories, posted in public, were really private messages of reproach from one man to the other. Sometimes the Dystopianist wondered if he were in fact the *only* reader the Dire Utopianist had, and the only one he wanted.

The cabbages were hopeless, the Dystopianist saw now.

Gazing out the window over his coffee's last plume of steam at the humming, pencil-colored school buses, he suddenly understood the gross implausibility: a rapidly inflating cabbage could never have the *stopping power* to *alter the fatal trajectory* of a *careening steel egg carton full of young lives*. A cabbage might halt a Hyundai, maybe a Volvo. Never a school bus. Anyway, the cabbages as an image had no implications, no *reach*. They said nothing about mankind. They were, finally, completely stupid and lame. He gulped the last of his coffee, angrily.

He had to go deeper, find something resonant, something to crawl beneath the skin of reality and render it monstrous from within. He paced to the sink, began rinsing his coffee mug. A tiny pod of silt had settled at the bottom and now, under a jet of cold tap water, the grains rose and spread and danced, a model of chaos. The Dystopianist retraced his seed of inspiration: *well-intentioned, bumbling geneticist*, good. Good enough. The geneticist needed to stumble onto something better, though.

One day, when the Dystopianist and the Dire Utopianist had been in the sixth grade at Intermediate School 293, cowering together in a corner of the schoolyard to duck sports and fights and girls in one deft multipurpose cower, they had arrived at a safe island of mutual interest: comic books, Marvel brand, which anyone who read them understood weren't comic at all but deadly, breathtakingly serious. Marvel constructed worlds of splendid complexity, full of chilling, ancient villains and tormented heroes, in richly unfinished story lines. There in the schoolyard, wedged for cover behind the girls' lunch-hour game of hopscotch, the Dystopianist declared his favorite character: Doctor Doom, antagonist of the Fantastic Four. Doctor Doom wore a forest green cloak and hood over a metallic slitted mask and armor. He was a dark king who from his gnarled castle ruled a city of hapless serfs. An imperial, self-righteous monster. The Dire Utopianist murmured his consent. Indeed, Doctor Doom was awesome, an honorable choice. The Dystopianist waited for the Dire Utopianist to declare his favorite.

"Black Bolt," said the Dire Utopianist.

The Dystopianist was confused. Black Bolt wasn't a villain or a hero. Black Bolt was part of an outcast band of mutant characters known as the Inhumans, the noblest among them. He was their leader, but he never spoke. His only *demonstrated* power was flight, but the whole point of Black Bolt was the power he restrained himself from using: speech. The sound of his voice was cataclysmic, an unusable weapon, like an atomic bomb. If Black Bolt ever uttered a syllable the world would crack in two. Black Bolt was leader in absentia much of the time—he had a tendency to exile himself from the scene, to wander distant mountaintops contemplating . . . What? His curse? The things he would say if he could safely speak?

It was an unsettling choice there, amidst the feral shrieks of the schoolyard. The Dystopianist changed the subject, and never raised the question of Marvel Comics with the Dire Utopianist again. Alone behind the locked door of his bedroom the Dystopianist studied Black Bolt's behavior, seeking hints of the character's appeal to his schoolmate. Perhaps the answer lay in a story line elsewhere in the Marvel universe, one where Black Bolt shucked off his pensiveness to function as an unrestrained hero or villain. If so, the Dystopianist never found the comic book in question.

Suicide, the Dystopianist concluded now. The geneticist should be studying suicide, seeking to isolate it as a factor in the human genome. "The Sylvia Plath Code," that might be the title of the story. The geneticist could be trying to *reproduce it in a nonhuman species*. Right, good. To breed for suicide in animals, to produce a creature with the impulse to take its own life. That had the relevance the Dystopianist was looking for. What animals? Something poignant and pathetic, something pure. Sheep. *The Sylvia Plath Sheep*, that was it.

A variant of sheep had been bred for the study of suicide. The Sylvia Plath Sheep had to be kept on close watch, like a prisoner stripped of sharp implements, shoelaces, and belt. And the Plath Sheep escapes, right, of course, *a Frankenstein creature always escapes*, but the twist is that the Plath Sheep is dangerous only to itself. *So what?* What harm if a single sheep quietly, discreetly offs itself? *But the Plath Sheep*, scribbling fingers racing now, the Dystopianist was on fire, *the Plath Sheep turns out to have the gift of communicating its despair*. Like the monkeys on that island, who learned from one another to wash clams, or break them open with coconuts, whatever it was the monkeys had learned, look into it later, *the Plath Sheep evoked suicide in other creatures*, all up and down the food chain. Not humans, but anything else that crossed its path. Cats, dogs, cows, beetles, clams. Each creature would spread suicide to another, to five or six others, before *searching out a promontory from which to plunge to its death*. The human species would be powerless to reverse the craze, the epidemic of suicide among the nonhuman species of the planet.

Okay! Right! Let goddamn Black Bolt open his mouth and sing an aria—he couldn't halt the Plath Sheep in its *deadly spiral of despair!*

The Dystopianist suddenly had a vision of the Plath Sheep wandering its way into the background of one of the Dire One's tales. It would go unremarked at first, a bucolic detail. Unwrapping its bleak gift of *global animal suicide* only after it had been taken entirely for granted, just as the Dire One's own little nuggets of despair were smuggled innocuously into his utopias. The Plath Sheep was a bullet of pure dystopian intention. The Dystopianist wanted to fire it in the Dire Utopianist's direction. Maybe he'd send this story to *Encouraging*.

Even better, he'd like it if he could send the Plath Sheep itself to the door of the Dire One's writing room. *Here's your tragic mute Black Bolt, you bastard!* Touch its somber muzzle, dry its moist obsidian eyes, runny with sleep goo. Try to talk it down from the parapet, if you have the courage of your ostensibly rosy convictions. Explain to the Sylvia Plath Sheep why life is worth living. Or, failing that, let the sheep convince you to follow it up to the brink, and go. You and the sheep, pal, take a fall.

There was a knock on the door.

The Dystopianist went to the door and opened it. Standing in the corridor was a sheep. The Dystopianist checked his watch—nine forty-five. He wasn't sure why it mattered to him what time it was, but it did. He found it reassuring. The day still stretched before him; he'd have plenty of time to resume work after this interruption. He still heard the children's voices leaking in through the front window from the street below. The children arriving now were late for school. There were always hundreds who were late. He wondered if the sheep had waited with the children for the crossing guard to wave it on. He wondered if the sheep had crossed at the green, or recklessly dared the traffic to kill it.

He'd persuaded himself that the sheep was voiceless. So it was a shock when it spoke. "May I come in?" said the sheep.

"Yeah, sure," said the Dystopianist, fumbling his words. Should he offer the sheep the couch, or a drink of something? The sheep stepped into the apartment, just far enough to allow the door to be closed behind it, then stood quietly working its nifty little jaw back and forth, and blinking. Its eyes were not watery at all.

"So," said the sheep, nodding its head at the Dystopianist's desk, the mass of yellow legal pads, the sharpened pencils bunched in their holder, the typewriter. "This is where the magic happens." The sheep's tone was wearily sarcastic.

"It isn't usually *magic*," said the Dystopianist, then immediately regretted the remark.

"Oh, I wouldn't say that," said the sheep, apparently unruffled. "You've got a few things to answer for."

"Is that what this is?" said the Dystopianist. "Some kind of reckoning?"

"Reckoning?" The sheep blinked as though confused. "Who said anything about a reckoning?"

"Never mind," said the Dystopianist. He didn't want to put words into the sheep's mouth. Not now. He'd let it represent itself, and try to be patient.

But the sheep didn't speak, only moved in tiny, faltering steps on the carpet, advancing very slightly into the room. The Dystopianist wondered if the sheep might be scouting for sharp corners on the furniture, for chances to do itself harm by butting with great force against his fixtures.

"Are you—very depressed?" asked the Dystopianist.

The sheep considered the question for a moment. "I've had better days, let's put it that way."

Finishing the thought, it stared up at him, eyes still dry. The Dystopianist met its gaze, then broke away. A terrible thought occurred to him: the sheep might be expecting *him* to relieve it of its life.

The silence was ponderous. The Dystopianist considered another possibility. Might his rival have come to him in disguised form?

He cleared his throat before speaking. "You're not, ah, the Dire One, by any chance?" The Dystopianist was going to be awfully embarrassed if the sheep didn't know what he was talking about.

The sheep made a solemn, wheezing sound, like

Hurrrrhh. Then it said, "I'm *dire* all right. But I'm hardly the only one."

"Who?" blurted the Dystopianist.

"Take a look in the mirror, friend."

"What's your point?" The Dystopianist was sore now. If the sheep thought he was going to be manipulated into suicide it had *another think coming*.

"Just this: How many sheep have to die to assuage your childish resentments?" Now the sheep assumed an odd false tone, bluff like that of a commercial pitchman: *"They laughed when I sat down at the Dystopiano! But when I began to play—"*

"Very funny."

"We try, we try. Look, could you at least offer me a dish of water or something? I had to take the stairs—couldn't reach the button for the elevator."

Silenced, the Dystopianist hurried into the kitchen and filled a shallow bowl with water from the tap. Then, thinking twice, he poured it back into the sink and replaced it with mineral water from the bottle in the door of his refrigerator. When he set it out the sheep lapped gratefully, steadily, seeming to the Dystopianist an animal at last.

"Okay." It licked its lips. "That's it, Doctor Doom. I'm out of here. Sorry for the intrusion, next time I'll call. I just wanted, you know—a look at you."

The Dystopianist couldn't keep from saying, "You don't want to die?"

"Not today," was the sheep's simple reply. The Dystopianist stepped carefully around the sheep to open the door, and the sheep trotted out. The Dystopianist trailed it into the corridor and summoned the elevator. When the cab arrived and the door opened the Dystopianist leaned in and punched the button for the lobby.

"Thanks," said the sheep. "It's the little things that count."

The Dystopianist tried to think of a proper farewell, but couldn't before the elevator door shut. The sheep was facing the rear of the elevator cab, another instance of its poor grasp of etiquette.

Still, the sheep's visit wasn't the worst the Dystopianist could imagine. It could have attacked him, or tried to gore itself on his kitchen knives. The Dystopianist was still proud of the Plath Sheep, and rather glad to have met it, even if the Plath Sheep wasn't proud of him. Besides, the entire episode had only cost the Dystopianist an hour or so of his time. He was back at work, eagerly scribbling out implications, extrapolations, another illustrious downfall, well before the yelping children reoccupied the schoolyard at lunchtime.

Super Goat Man

WHEN SUPER GOAT MAN MOVED INTO THE commune on our street I was ten years old. Though I liked superheroes, I wasn't familiar with Super Goat Man. His presence didn't mean anything, particularly, to myself or to the other kids in the neighborhood. For us, as we ran and screamed and played secret games on the sidewalk, Super Goat Man was only another of the men who sat on stoops in sleeveless undershirts on hot summer days, watching the slow progress of life on the block. The two little fleshy horns on his forehead didn't make him especially interesting. We weren't struck by his fall from grace, out of the world of comic-book heroes, among which he had been at best a minor star, to land here in Cobble Hill, Brooklyn, in a single room in what was basically a dorm for college dropouts, a hippie group shelter, any more than we were by the tufts of extra hair at his throat and behind his ears. We had eyes only for Spider-Man or Batman in those days, superheroes in two dimensions, with lunch boxes and television shows and theme songs. Super Goat Man had none of those.

It was our dads who cared. They were unmistakably drawn to the strange figure who'd moved to the block, as though for them he represented some lost possibility in their own lives. My father in particular seemed fascinated with Super Goat Man, though he covered this interest by acting as though it were on my behalf. One day toward the end of that summer he and I walked to Montague Street, to visit the comics shop there. This was a tiny storefront filled with long white boxes, crates full of carefully archived comics, protected by plastic bags and cardboard backing. The boxes contained ancient runs of back issues of titles I'd heard of, as well as thousands of other comics featuring characters I'd never encountered. The shop was presided over by a nervous young pedant with long hair and a beard, a collector-type himself, an old man in spirit who distrusted children in his store, as he ought to have. He assisted my father in finding what he sought, deep in the alphabetical archive—a five-issue run of *The Remarkable Super Goat Man*, from Electric Comics. These were the only comics in which Super Goat Man had appeared. There were just five issues because after five the title had been forever canceled. My father seemed satisfied with what he'd found. We paid for the five issues and left.

I didn't know how to explain to my father that Electric wasn't one of the major comics publishers. The stories the comics contained, when we inspected them together, were both ludicrous and boring. Super Goat Man's five issues showed him rescuing old ladies from swerving trucks and kittens from lightning-struck trees, and battling dull villains like Vest Man and False Dave. The drawings were amateurish, cut-rate, antiquated. I couldn't have articulated these judgments then, of course. I only knew I disliked the comics, found them embarrassing, for myself, for Super Goat Man, and for my dad. They languished in my room, unread, and were eventually cleaned up—I mean, thrown out—by my mom.

For the next few years Super Goat Man was less than a minor curiosity to me. I didn't waste thought on him. The younger men and women who lived in the commune took him for granted, as anyone should, so far as I knew. We kids would see him in their company, moving furniture up the stoop and into the house, discarded dressers and couches and lamps they'd found on the street, or taping posters on lampposts announcing demonstrations against nuclear power or in favor of day-care centers, or weeding in the commune's pathetic front yard, which was intended as a vegetable garden but was choked not only with uninvited growth but with discarded ice-cream wrappers and soda bottles—we kids used the commune's yard as a dumping ground. It didn't occur to me that Super Goat

Man was much older, really, than the commune's other oc-
cupants, that in fact they might be closer to my age than
to his. However childish their behavior, the hippies all
seemed as dull and remote as grown-ups to me.

It was the summer when I was thirteen that my parents
allowed me to accompany them to one of the commune's
potluck dinners. The noise and vibrancy of that house's
sporadic celebrations were impossible to ignore on our
street, and I knew my parents had attended a few earlier
parties—warily, I imagined. The inhabitants of the commune were always trying to sweep their neighbors into dubious causes, and it might be a mistake to be seduced by
frivolity into some sticky association. But my parents liked
fun too. And had too little of it. Their best running jokes
concerned the dullness of their friends' dinner parties.
This midsummer evening they brought me along to see inside the life of the scandalous, anomalous house.

The house was already full, many bearded and jeweled
and scruffy, reeking of patchouli and musk, others, like
my parents, dressed in their hippest collarless shirts and
paisley blouses, wearing their fattest beads and bracelets.
The offerings, nearly all casseroles brimming with exotic
gray proteins, beans and tofu and eggplant and more I
couldn't name, were lined on a long side table, mostly ignored. This was a version of cocktail hour, with beer
drunk from the bottle and well-rolled marijuana cigarettes. I didn't see whether my parents indulged in the latter. My mother accepted a glass of orange juice, surely
spiked. I meant not to pay them any attention, so I moved

for the stairs. There were partiers leaning on the banister at the first landing, and evidence of music playing in upstairs rooms, so I didn't doubt the whole house was open to wandering.

There was no music coming from the garden-facing room on the second floor, but the door was open and three figures were visible inside, seated on cushions on a mattress on the floor. A young couple, and Super Goat Man. From his bare hairy feet on the mattress, I guessed it was his room I'd entered. The walls were sparse apart from a low bookcase, on which I spotted, laid crosswise in the row of upright spines, Norman Mailer's *Armies of the Night*, Sergei Eisenstein's *Film Form / The Film Sense*, and Thomas Pynchon's *V*. The three titles stuck in my head; I would later attempt to read each of the three at college, succeeding only with the Mailer. Beside the bookcase was a desk heaped with papers, and behind it a few black-and-white postcards had been thumbtacked to the wall. These looked less like a considered decoration than as if they'd been pinned up impulsively by a sitter at the desk. One of the postcard images I recognized as Charlie Parker, clutching a saxophone with his meaty hands. The jazzman was an idol of my father's, perhaps a symbol of his vanished youth.

The young man on the mattress was holding a book: *Memories, Dreams, Reflections*, by Carl Jung. Super Goat Man had evidently just pressed it on him, and had likely been extolling its virtues when I walked into the room.

"Hello," said the young woman, her voice warm. I must

have been staring, from my place in the middle of the room.

"You're Everett, aren't you?" said Super Goat Man, before I could speak.

"How'd you know my name?"

"You live on the block," said Super Goat Man. "I've seen you running around."

"I think we'll head down, Super Goat Man," said the young man abruptly, tucking the book under his arm as he got up from the mattress. "Get something to eat before it's too late."

"I want to hit the dance floor," said the young woman.

"See you down there," said Super Goat Man. With that the young couple were gone.

"You checking out the house?" said Super Goat Man to me once we were alone. "Casing the joint?"

"I'm looking for my friend," I lied.

"I think some kids are hanging out in the backyard."

"No, she went upstairs." I wanted him to think I had a girlfriend.

"Okay, cool," said Super Goat Man. He smiled. I suppose he was waiting for me to leave, but he didn't give any sign that I was bothering him by staying.

"Why do you live here?" I asked.

"These are my friends," he said. "They helped me out when I lost my job."

"You're not a superhero anymore, are you?"

Super Goat Man shrugged. "Some people felt I was

being too outspoken about the war. Anyway, I wanted to accomplish things on a more local level."

"Why don't you have a secret identity?"

"I wasn't that kind of superhero."

"But what was your name, before?"

"Ralph Gersten."

"What did Ralph Gersten do?"

"He was a college teacher, for a couple of years."

"So why aren't you Ralph Gersten now?"

"Sometime around when they shot Kennedy I just realized Ralph Gersten wasn't who I was. He was a part of an old life I was holding on to. So I became Super Goat Man. I've come to understand that this is who I am, for better or worse."

This was a bit much for me to assimilate, so I changed the subject. "Do you smoke pot?"

"Sometimes."

"Were Mr. and Mrs. Gersten sad when you gave up your secret identity?"

"Who?"

"Your parents."

Super Goat Man smiled. "They weren't my real parents. I was adopted."

Suddenly I was done. "I'm going downstairs, Super Goat Man."

"Okay, Everett," he said. "See you down there, probably."

I made my way downstairs, and lurked in the commune's muddy and ill-lit backyard, milling with the other teenagers and children stranded there by the throngs of frolickers—for the party was now overflowing its bounds, and we were free to steal beers from the counter and carry on our own tentative party, our own fumbling flirtations. I had no girlfriend, but I did play spin the bottle that night, crouched on the ground beneath a fig tree.

Then, near midnight, I went back inside. The living room was jammed with bodies—dancers on a parquet floor that had been revealed when the vast braided rug had been curled up against the base of the mantel. Colored Christmas lights were bunched in the corner, and some of them blinked to create a gently eerie strobe. I smelled sweat and smoke. Feeling perverse and thrilled by the kisses I'd exchanged in the mud beneath the tree, I meandered into the web of celebrants.

Super Goat Man was there. He was dancing with my mother. She was as I'd never seen her, braceleted wrists crossed above her head, swaying to the reggae—I think it was the sound track to *The Harder They Come.* Super Goat Man was more dressed-up than he'd been in his room upstairs. He wore a felt brocade vest and striped pants. He danced in tiny little steps, almost as though losing and regaining his balance, his arms loose at his sides, fingers snapping. Mostly he moved his head to the beat, shaking it back and forth as if saying *no-no-no, no-no-no.* He shook his head at my mother's dancing, as if he couldn't approve of the way she was moving, but couldn't quit paying attention either.

My father? He was seated on the rolled-up rug, his back against the mantel, elbows on his knees, dangling with forefinger and thumb a nearly empty paper cup of red wine. Like me, he was watching my mom and Super Goat Man. It didn't look as if it bothered him at all.

    •   •   •

MY JUNIOR year at Corcoran College, in Corcoran, New Hampshire, Super Goat Man was brought in to fill the Walt Whitman Chair in the Humanities. This was 1981, the dawn of Reagan. The chair was required to offer one course; Super Goat Man's was listed in the catalogue as Dissidence and Desire: Marginal Heroics in American Life 1955–1975. The reading included Frantz Fanon, Roland Barthes, and Timothy Leary. It was typical of Corcoran that it would choose that particular moment to recuperate a figure associated with sixties protest, to enshrine what had once been at the vigorous center of the culture in the harmless pantheon of academia. It was Super Goat Man's first teaching job since the fifties. The commune on our street had shut down at some point in my high-school years, and I don't know where Super Goat Man had been in the intervening time. I certainly hadn't thought about him since departing for college.

He'd gained a little weight, but was otherwise unchanged. I first spotted him moving across the Commons lawn on a September afternoon, one with the scent of fallen and fermenting crab apples on the breeze. It was one of those rare, sweet days on either side of the long New Hampshire winter, when a school year was either falsely fresh before its plunge into bleak December, or exhausted and ready to give way to summer. Super Goat Man wore a forest green corduroy suit and a wide salmon tie, but his feet were still bare. A couple of Corcoran girls trailed alongside him. He had a book open as he walked—perhaps he was reading them a poem.

The college had assigned Super Goat Man one of the dormitory apartments—a suite of rooms built into Sweeney House, one of the student residences. That is to say, he lived on the edge of the vast commons lawn, and we students felt his watchful presence much as I had in Cobble Hill, on our street. I didn't take Super Goat Man's class, which was mostly full of freshmen, and of those renegade history and rhetoric majors who'd been seduced by French strains of philosophy and literary theory. I fancied myself a classics scholar then—though I'd soon divert into a major in history—and wasn't curious about contemporary political theory, even if I'd believed Super Goat Man to be a superior teacher, which I didn't. I wasn't certain he had nothing to offer the Corcoran students, but whatever it might be it wasn't summed up by the title of his class.

I did, however, participate in one of the late-night salons in the living room of Sweeney House. Super Goat Man had begun appearing there casually, showing up after a few students had occupied the couches, and had lit a fire or opened a bottle of red wine. Increasingly his presence was relied upon; soon it was a given that he was the center of an unnamed tradition. Though Corcoran College was then in the throes of a wave of glamorous eighties-style binge parties, and cocaine had begun to infiltrate our sanctum in the New Hampshire woods as if we were all denizens of Andy Warhol's Factory, the Sweeney House salons were a throwback to another, earlier temperature of college socializing. Bearded art students who disdained dancing in favor of bull sessions, Woolfian-Plathian girls in long antique dresses, and lonely gay virgins of both genders—these were the types who found their way to Sweeney to sit at Super Goat Man's feet. There were also, from what I observed, a handful of quiet superhero comic-book fans who revered Super Goat Man in that capacity and were covertly basking in his aura, ashamed to ask the sorts of questions I'd peppered him with in his room in the communal house, so long ago.

The evening I sat in, Super Goat Man had dragged his phonograph out from his apartment and set it up in the living room so that he could play Lenny Bruce records for his acolytes. Super Goat Man had five or six of the records. He spoke intermittently, his voice unhurried and reflective, explaining the context of the famous comedian's arrests and courtroom battles before dropping the needle on a given track. After a while conversation drifted to other subjects. Cross talk arose, though whenever Super Goat Man began to speak in his undemonstrative way all chatter fell deferentially silent. Then Super Goat Man went into his apartment and brought out an Ornette Coleman LP.

"You know a bit about jazz, don't you, Everett?" It was the first time he'd addressed me directly. I hadn't known he'd recognized me.

"A thing or two, I guess."

"Everett's father was the one who turned me on to Rahsaan Roland Kirk," Super Goat Man told a teenager I recognized, a bespectacled sophomore who'd impressively talked his way into a classics seminar that was meant for upperclassmen. "I always thought that stuff was too gimmicky, but I'd never really listened."

I tried to imagine when Super Goat Man and my dad had spent so much time together. It was almost impossible to picture, but Super Goat Man didn't have any reason to be lying about it. It was one of the first times I was forced to consider the possibility that my parents had social lives—that they had lives.

"Does your father write about jazz?" the sophomore asked me, wide-eyed. I suppose he'd misunderstood Super Goat Man's remark. There were plenty of famous—or at least interesting—fathers at Corcoran College, but mine wasn't one of them.

"My father works for New York State," I said. "Department of Housing and Urban Development. Well, he just lost his job, in fact."

"He's a good five-card-stud player too," said Super

Goat Man. "Cleaned me out a few times, I don't mind saying."

"Oh yeah, my dad's a real supervillain," I said with the heaviest sarcasm I could muster. I was embarrassed to think of my father sucking up to Super Goat Man, as he surely had during their long evenings together, whoever had taken the bulk of the chips.

Then the squeaky jazz began playing, and Super Goat Man, though seated in one of the dormitory's ratty armchairs, closed his eyes and began shaking his head as if transported back to the commune's dance floor, or perhaps to some even earlier time. I studied his face. The tufts around his ears and throat were graying. I puzzled over his actual age. Had Super Goat Man once spent decades frozen in a block of ice, like Captain America? If Ralph Gersten had been a college teacher in the fifties, he was probably older than my dad.

Eight months later the campus was green again. The term was almost finished, all of us nearly freed to summer, when it happened: the incident at the Campanile. A Saturday, late in a balmy night of revels, the Commons lawn full of small groups crossing from dorm to dorm, cruising at the parties which still flared like bonfires in the landscape of the campus. Many of us yet owed papers, others would have to sit in a final class the following Monday, but the mood was one of expulsive release from our labors. It was nearly three in the morning when Rudy Krugerrand and Seth Brummell, two of the wealthiest and most widely reviled frat boys at Corcoran, scaled the Campanile tower and began bellowing.

I was among those awake and near enough by to be drawn by the commotion, into the small crowd at the dark base of the Campanile tower. When I first gazed up at Rudy and Seth I was confused by what I saw: Were there four figures spotlit against the clock beneath the bells? And where were the campus authorities? It was as though this night had been officially ceded to some bacchanalian imperative.

That spring a sculpture student had, as his thesis project, decorated the Commons with oversize office supplies—a stapler in the dimensions of a limousine, a log painted as a number two pencil, and a pile of facsimile paper clips each the height of a human being, fashioned out of plastic piping and silver paint. I suppose the work was derivative of Claes Oldenburg, but the result made an impressive spectacle. It was two of the paper-clip sculptures that Rudy Krugerrand and Seth Brummell had managed to attach to their belts like mannequin dance partners and drag with them out onto the ledge of the Campanile clock, where they stood now, six stories from the ground. On the precipice at the clockface, their faces uplit in the floodlights, Rudy and Seth were almost like players in the climax of some Gothic silent-film drama, but they didn't have the poise or imagination to know it. They were only college pranksters, reelingly drunk, Seth with a three-quarters empty bottle of Jack Daniels still in his hand, and at first it was hard to make out what they were shouting.

We on the ground predictably shouted *"Jump!"* back at them, knowing they loved themselves too dearly ever to consider it.

Then Rudy Krugerrand's slurred voice rose out above the din—or perhaps it was only that I picked it out of the din for the first time. "Calling Super Goat Man! Calling Super Goat Man!" He shouted this until his voice broke hoarse. "This looks like a job for Super Goat Man! Come out, come out, wherever you are!"

"What's going on?" I asked a student beside me.

He shrugged. "I guess they're calling out Super Goat Man. They want to see if he can get them down from the ledge."

"What do you mean?"

"They want to see him use his powers."

From the clock tower Seth Brummell screamed now, in a girlish falsetto: "Oh, Super Goat Man, where are you?"

A stirring had begun in the crowd, which had grown by now to a hundred or more. A murmuring. Super Goat Man's name was planted like a seed. Under the guise of concern for Rudy and Seth, but certainly with a shiver of voyeuristic anticipation, some had begun to speak of going to the Sweeney House apartment, to see if Super Goat Man could be located. There was a hint of outrage: Why wasn't he here already? What kind of Super Goat Man was he, anyway?

Now a group of fifteen or twenty broke out and streamed down the hill, toward Sweeney House. Others trailed after them, myself included. I hid in this crowd, feeling like an observer, though I suppose I was as complicit as anyone. Were we only curious, or a part of a mob? It seemed, anyway, that we were under the direction of Rudy and Seth.

"That's right," mocked Rudy. "Only Super Goat Man can save us now!"

Those who'd led the charge hammered on Super Goat Man's apartment door for a good few minutes before getting a result. Bold enough to have woken him, they inched backward at the sight of him on his threshold, dressed only in a flowery silk kimono, blinking groggily at the faces arrayed on the hill. Then someone stepped forward and took his arm, pointed him toward the Campanile. Any conversation was drowned in murmurs, and by the sound of sirens, now belatedly pulling up at the base of the tower. Super Goat Man shook his head sorrowfully, but he began to trek up the hill to the Commons, toward the Campanile. We all fell in around and behind him, emboldened at marching to the beat of a superhero's step, feeling the pulse of the script it now appeared would be played out, ignoring the fact that it had been written by Rudy and Seth and Jack Daniels. Super Goat Man's kimono fluttered slightly, not quite a cape. He tightened the sash, and strode, rubbing at his eyes with balled fists.

This success only seemed to enrage Rudy and Seth, who writhed and scorned from atop their perch. "Baaahh, baaahh, Super Goat Man!" they roared. "What's the matter with your goaty senses? Smoke too much dope tonight? *Fuck* you, Super Goat Man!" Seth lifted his giant paper clip above his head, to shake it like a fake strongman's prop dumbbell.

The campus police began to herd the students from the base of the tower, but our arriving throng pushed the opposite way. In the confusion, the young policemen seemed utterly helpless, and fell back. Straining on tiptoe to see over the heads of the crowd, I followed the progress of the lime green kimono as Super Goat Man was thrust to the fore, not necessarily by his own efforts. Above, Seth was strumming air-guitar chords on his paper clip, then waggling it over our heads like an enormous phallus.

"Bite my crank, Super Goat Man!"

The crowd gasped as Super Goat Man shed his garb— for mobility I suppose—and started shimmying, almost scampering, up the face of the tower. His pelt was glossy in the moonlight, but nobody could have mistaken the wide swath of white above his dusky buttocks for sheen. Super Goat Man was aging. He scurried through the leaf-blobby shade a tree branch cast against the side of the tower, then back into the light. Whether it was the pressure of expectation on a still-sleepy mind, or possibly a genuine calling to heroics, a hope he could do some good here, Super Goat Man had taken the bait. His limbs worked miraculously in ascending the tower, yet one could only dread what would come if he reached the idiot boys at the top, who grew more agitated and furious at every inch he achieved. Rudy had lifted his own paper clip, to match Seth, and now he swung it out over us.

The plummet silenced us. It was over before we could

swallow our words and form a cry to replace them. Six stories is no distance at all, only enough. Rudy's paper clip had overbalanced him. Super Goat Man had braced three limbs, and reached out with a fourth—some number of us saw, others only imagined afterward—but he didn't come away with Rudy. Super Goat Man caught the paper clip in mid-flight with the prehensile toes of his left foot, and the sculpture was jerked free from Rudy as he fell. That's how firm was Super Goat Man's hold on the tower's third story: it was left for later to speculate whether he might have been able to halt a human body's fall. Rudy came to earth, shattering at the feet of the policemen there at the tower's base. Now the nude furry figure could only undertake a sober, methodical descent, paper clip tucked beneath one arm. At the clockface, Seth Brummell was mute, clinging to a post, to wait for the security men who would soon unlock the small door in the tower behind him and angrily yank him to safety.

Rudy Krugerrand survived his fall. His ruined spine cost him the use of his legs, cost him all feeling below some point at his middle. Only a junior, he rather courageously reappeared in a mechanical wheelchair the following September, resumed his studies, resumed drinking too, though his temperament was mellowed, reflective now. He'd be seen at parties dozing in the corner after the dance floor had filled—it took very little beer to knock his dwindled body out. If Rudy had died, or never returned, the incident likely would have been avidly discussed, etched into campus legend. Instead it was covered in a clumsy hush.

The coexistence in the same small community of Rudy and Super Goat Man—who'd been offered a seat in the social sciences, and accepted—comprised a kind of odd, insoluble puzzle: Had the hero failed the crisis? Caused it, by some innate provocation? Or was the bogus crisis unworthy, and the outcome its own reward? Who'd shamed whom?

I contemplated this koan, or didn't, for just another year. My graduate studies took me to the University of California at Irvine, three thousand grateful miles from Corcoran, now Super Goat Man's province. I didn't see him, or think of him again, for more than a decade.

• • •

THE SWEETEST student I ever had was an Italian girl named Angela Verucci. Tall, bronze-skinned, with a quizzical, slightly humorless cast, dressed no matter the weather in neat pantsuits or skirts with stockings, in heavy tortoise-shell glasses frames and with her blond hair knit in a tight, almost Japanese bun, her aura of seriousness and her Mediterranean luster outshone the blandly cornfed and T-shirted students in whose midst she had materialized. Angela Verucci was not so much a girl, really: twenty-four years old, she'd already studied at Oxford before taking the Reeves Fellowship that had brought her to America. She spoke immaculate English, and though her accreditation was a mess, truly she was nearly as accomplished a medievalist as I was the day she appeared in my class. This was at Oregon State University, in Corvallis, where I'd been given a two-year postdoc after my six years at Irvine. Oregon State was the third stop in Angela Verucci's American tour—she'd also spent a year at Columbia and, as it happened, a term at Corcoran.

What does a single, thirty-year-old history professor do with the sweetest student he's ever had? He waits until the end of the semester, files a Circular of Intent with the Faculty Appropriateness Committee, and in early spring asks her to hike with him to the highest point in the county, a lookout over three mountain ranges called Sutter's Parlor. Angela Verucci arrived in heels, perhaps not completely grasping the sense of the invitation. We forsook the ascent in favor of a glass of Oregon Pinot Noir on a restaurant patio perched on the Willamette River—near enough, for the Brooklynite and the Sicilian, to an expedition.

We were married two years later, on the Italian island itself. The ceremony was deferentially Catholic; I didn't care. The wider circle of my acquaintances learned the happy details in a mass e-mail. Then Angela and I returned to our quiet rented bungalow in New Brunswick, New Jersey. I was at Rutgers then, on a second postdoc, and hungry for a tenure-track position. My job interviews were hardly unsuccessful: I was never summarily dismissed, instead always called back for second and third visits, always asked to teach a sample class. Afterward, polite notes flew back and forth, candidate and committee reassuring one another of how fine the experience had been, how glad we both were to have met. Only I never got a job.

So by the time I got the invitation to interview for a position at Corcoran, the New England pastures of my alma mater didn't appear such a poor fate. It was the week of Halloween, the weather glorious, so at the very least the day of the interview would be a nice jaunt. We left early, to roam a few New Hampshire back roads, then ate a picnic lunch beside Corcoran Pond before I checked in for an afternoon of meetings.

Corcoran looked implacable, though I knew it was changed. The school had been through financial shake-ups and tenure scandals; those had, in turn, purged most of the administrators and faculty I'd known. But the grounds, the crab apple trees and white clapboard, were eternal as a country-store calendar. While Angela took a memory tour, heading for her old dorm, I turned up for my scheduled tribunal. There, I was debriefed by peers, a couple of them younger than myself. The room was full of the usual tensions: some of these people had an investment in my candidacy, some had bets on other tables. No one was in the least sentimental about my status as alumnus—that was reserved, I supposed, for the dinner tonight, arranged in my honor at the president's house. After a finishing round of polite handclasps I was ferried to the president's office. On top of tonight's dinner, she'd also wanted to meet me alone. I figured it was a good sign.

The president asked how I'd liked the interview; we

made this and other small talk. She asked about my years at Corcoran, which I painted in rosy tones. Then she said: "Did you know Super Goat Man when you were a student here?"

"Sure," I said. "I mean, I never took a class with him."

"He surprised me by asking to join us at the dinner tonight—he usually doesn't bother with faculty socializing anymore."

"He's still here?" I was amazed Super Goat Man, of all people, had threaded his way through so many personnel shake-ups.

"Yes, though he's reduced to a kind of honorary presence. He doesn't actually teach now. I don't know if he'd be capable of it. But he's beloved. The students joke that he can be spotted strolling across Commons lawn twice a semester. And that if you want to get any time with him, you can join him on the stroll."

"He recognized my name?"

"He seemed to, yes. You should prepare yourself. He's quite infirm."

"How—how old is he?"

"Measured in years, I don't know. But there's been an accelerated aging process. You'll see."

Perhaps superheroism was a sort of toxin, like a steroid, one with a punitive cost to the body. I mused on this as I departed the president's office, crossed the Commons, and headed through the parking lot and downhill, to find the bench beside Corcoran Creek, a favorite spot, where Angela had said she'd wait. I saw my wife before she saw me, her feet tucked up on the slats, abandoned shoes beneath, her body curled around a big hardback biography of Rousseau. In the distance, dying October light drew long saddle-shaped curves on the White Mountains of New Hampshire. Suddenly I could picture us here for a long time, and picture it happily.

"How did it go?" she asked when she noticed me.

"Par: two friends, two enemies, one sleeper."

"And the president?"

"Nice, but she wasn't giving anything away." I put my hands on her shoulders. She closed the book.

"You seem distant," Angela said. "Memories?"

"Yes." In fact, I was thinking about Super Goat Man. I'd never before considered the sacrifice he'd made, enunciating his political views so long ago. Fruitlessly, it seemed to me. In exchanging his iconic, trapped-in-amber status, what had he gained? Had Super Goat Man really accomplished much outside the parameters of his comics? However unglamorous the chores, didn't kittens *need* rescuing from trees? Didn't Vest Man require periodic defeating? Why jettison Ralph Gersten if in the end all you attained was life as a campus mascot?

I wanted to convey some of this to Angela, but didn't know where to begin. "When you were here—" I began, then stopped.

"Yes?"

"Did you know Super Goat Man?"

I felt her stiffen. "Of course, everybody knew him," she said.

"He's still here." I watched her as I spoke. Her gaze dipped to the ground.

"You saw him?"

"No, but we will at dinner tonight."

"How . . . unexpected." Now Angela was the one in fugue.

"Did you study with him?"

"He rarely taught. I attended a few talks."

"I thought you didn't like that stuff."

She shrugged. "I was curious."

I waited to understand. Crickets had begun a chorus in the grass. The sun ebbed. Soon we'd need to visit our bed-and-breakfast outside campus, to change into fresh clothes for the dinner party. Ordinarily such gatherings were clumsy at best, with grudges incompletely smothered under the surface of the talk, among tenured faculty who knew one another far too well. Something in me now curdled at the prospect of this one. In fact, I'd begun to dread it.

"Everett." There was something Angela wanted to tell me.

I made a preemptive guess. "Did you have some sort of something with Super Goat Man?" This was how she and I blundered through one another's past liaisons—we'd never been systematic.

I moved around the bench, to try and look her in the eye.

"Just an—affair. Nothing."

"What's nothing?"

She shrugged, and flipped her fingers as though dispelling a small fog. "We fooled around a few times. It was stupid."

I felt the poison of bitterness leach into my bloodstream. "I don't know why but I find that totally disgusting."

"Oh, Everett." Angela raised her arms, moved to assuage me, knowing as she did my visceral possessiveness, the bolt of jealousy that shot through me when contemplating her real past, anytime it arose. Of course, she couldn't understand my special history with Super Goat Man. How could she if I didn't? I'd never even mentioned him.

"I was a silly girl." She spoke gently. "And I didn't know you yet."

Unsatisfied, I wished her to declare that the encounter had been abusive, an ethical violation. Not that I had any ground to stand on. Anyway, she was Italian in this, as in all things. It was just an affair.

"Do you want to skip the dinner?"

She scowled. "That's silly. He wouldn't even remember. And I don't care. It's really nothing, my darling. My love."

At the president's house Super Goat Man was the last to arrive, so I was allowed to fantasize briefly that I'd been spared. The sight, when he did come in, was startling. He'd not only aged, but shrunk—I doubted if he was even five feet tall. He was, as ever, barefooted, and wore white muslin pajamas, with purple piping. The knees of the pajama bottoms were smudged with mud. As he entered the room, creeping in among us as we stood with our cocktail glasses, I quickly saw the reason for the smudges: as Super Goat Man's rickety steps faltered he dropped briefly to all fours. There, on the ground, he'd shake himself, almost like a wet dog. Then he'd rise again, on palsied limbs.

No one took notice of this. The guests, the other faculty, were inured, polite. In this halting manner Super Goat Man made his way past us, to the dining room. Apparently he wasn't capable of mingling, or even necessarily of speech. He took a seat at the long table, his bunched face, his squinting eyes and wrinkled horns, nearly at the level of his place setting. So Super Goat Man's arrival curtailed cocktail hour, as we began drifting in behind him, almost guiltily. The president's husband showed us to our places, which had been carefully designated, though an accommodation was evidently being made for Super Goat Man, who'd plopped down where he liked and wasn't to be budged. I was at the right hand of the president, and the left of the chair of the hiring committee. Again, a good sign. Angela sat across from me, Super Goat Man many places away, at the other end of the table.

I actually managed to forget him for the duration of the meal. He was, so far as I could tell, silent at his feed, and the women on either side of him turned to their other partners, or conversed across the width of the table. Toward the end we were served a course of cognac and dessert, and the president's husband passed around cigars, which he bragged were Cuban. Some of the women fled their chairs to avoid the smoke; other guests rose and mingled again in the corners of the room. It was in this interval of disarrangement that Super Goat Man pushed himself off his chair and made his way to the seat at my left, which the president had vacated. He had to collapse to his knees only once on the way, and he offered no evidence of sacrificed dignity as he rose from the floor.

Angela remained in her seat. Unlike any of the American women, she'd accepted a cigar, and now leaned it into the flame of a lighter proffered by an older professor she'd been entertaining throughout the meal. Her eyes found mine as Super Goat Man approached. Her expression was curious, and not unsympathetic.

Super Goat Man prodded my arm with a finger. I turned and considered him. Black pupils gleamed behind a hedge of eyebrows. His resplendent tufts had thinned and spread—the hair of his face had been redistributed, to form a merciful gauze across his withered features.

"I . . . knew . . . your . . . father." His voice was mossy, sepulchral.

"Yes," I said simply, keeping my voice low. No one was paying us any attention, yet. Not apart from Angela.

"You . . . remember . . . ?"

"Of course."

"We . . . love . . . jazz . . ."

I wondered whether he meant my father or, somehow, me. I had in fact over the years come around to my father's love of jazz, though my preference was not so much Ornette Coleman and Rahsaan Roland Kirk as Duke Ellington and Fletcher Henderson.

". . . poker . . ."

"He cleaned you out," I reminded him.

"Yezz . . . good times . . . beautiful women . . ." He struggled, swallowed hard, blinked. "All this controversy . . . not worth it . . ."

"My father was never involved in any controversy," I heard myself say, though I knew Super Goat Man was speaking only of himself, his lost career.

"No . . . absolutely true . . . knew how to live . . ."

Angela had leaned back, pursing her lips to savor the cigar. I might have noticed the room's gabble of conversation had dampened somewhat—might have noticed it sooner, I mean.

"So . . . many . . . hangovers . . ."

"But you and I have something in common besides my father," I told Super Goat Man.

"Yezz . . . yezz . . . ?"

"Of course we do," I began, and though I now understood we had the attention of the entire room, that the novelty of Super Goat Man's reminiscences had drawn every ear, I found myself unable to quit before I finished the thought. Further, having gained their attention, I allowed my voice to rise to a garrulous, plummy tone, as if I were starring in dinner theater. Before the line was half out of my mouth, I knew that the words, by airing the sort of laundry so desperately repressed in a community as precious as Corcoran, damned my candidacy. But that was a prize I no longer sought. Broader repercussions I could only guess at. My wife's eyes were on me now, her cigar's blunt tip flaring. I'd answer to her, later, if she gave me the chance.

It was the worst thing I could think to say. The impulse had formed in the grip of sexual jealousy, of course. But before it crossed my lips I knew my loathing had its origins in an even deeper place, the mind of a child wondering at his father's own susceptibility to the notion of a hero.

What I said was this: "I once saw you rescue a paper clip."

The
National Anthem

1/12/03

Dear M,

Our long letters are pleasing to me, but they do come
slowly. Lulled by the intrinsic properties of e-mail, I've
been willing to let most of my other correspondence slide
down that slippery slope, into hectic witty ping-pong. But
our deep connection, for twenty years or more now unre-
freshed or diluted or whatever it would be by regular com-
munications in person or on the phone, is precious to me,
and demands more traditional letters, even if those mean
long gaps. I suppose three-month breaks are not so much

in a friendship once treated so casually that we let nearly a decade go by, eh?

You asked about A. We've finally broken it off, the end of a nearly three-year chapter in my life, and a secret chapter as well. For, apart from you, safely remote in Japan, I've confided in no one. Her horrible marriage survived us, a fact that would have seemed absurd to me at the beginning, if some time traveler had come back to whisper it in my ear. The break was mutual—mutual enough to give it that name—and I'd be helpless to guess who is the more scarred. We won't be friends, but we were never going to be. Dissolving a secret affair is eerily simple: A and I only had to quit lying that we didn't exist.

Did I tell you about "The National Anthem"? I don't think so. This was the first night we stole together from her husband, the first intentional rendezvous, at a bed-and-breakfast outside Portland, Maine. A always traveled with a Walkman and a wallet of CDs, and that night, as we lay entwined in a twee canopy bed, she insisted on playing me a song, though there was no way for us to listen to it together. Instead she cued it up and watched me while it played, her ungroggy eyes inspecting me from below the horizon of my chest, mine a posture of submission: James Carr singing "The Dark End of the Street." I recognized it, but I'd never listened closely before. It's a song of infidelity and hopeless love, full of doomed certainty that the lovers, the love, will fail.

"I've got a friend who calls that 'The National Anthem,'" she said.

I gave her what was surely a weak-sickly smile, though likely I thought it was a cool and dispassionate one, at the time. She didn't elaborate, just let it sink in. I didn't ask who the friend might be—the unspecificity seemed as essential to the mood between us as the dual rental cars, the welcoming basket of cookies and fruit we'd ignored downstairs, or the silent fucking we'd enjoyed, our orgasms discrete, in turn. To press one another back into the world of names, of our real individual lives, would have seemed a rent in the shroud of worldly arbitrariness which enclosed our passion. Of course this was morbid, I see it now.

"There's a Bob Dylan song," I said then. " 'Ninety Miles an Hour (Down a Dead End Street).' I think it's a cover, actually. Same thing: *We're on a bad motorcycle with a devil in the seat, going ninety miles an hour down a dead end street . . .*"

"Yes, but this is 'The National Anthem.' "

By refusing the comparison A put me on notice that this wasn't a dialogue, but a preemptive declaration. She'd be the one to manage our yearnings, by her foreknowledge of despair. Fair enough: her jadedness was what I'd been drawn to in the first place.

Of course you know, M, because I've told you stories, how we rode her jadedness—our bad motorcycle—down our own dead-end street. It wasn't kept anonymously cute, with baskets of cookies, for long. The perversity of the affair, it seems to me now, is that under cover of delivering her from the marriage she claimed to be so tired of, A and I climbed inside the armature of that marriage instead. By skulking at its foundations, its skirts, we only proved its superiority. However aggrieved she and R might be, however dubious their prospect, it wasn't a secret affair, wasn't nearly as contemptible as *us*. Certainly that can be the only explanation for why, in a world of motels and with my own apartment free, we so often met at her place—at theirs. And I think now that though I mimed indifference whenever she predicted imminent destruction, I'd *lusted* to destroy a marriage, that I was far more interested in R than I allowed myself to know.

But I don't want to make this letter about A. You've written at length about your uncertainties in your own marriage—written poignantly, then switched to a tone of flippancy, as though to reassure me not to be too concerned. Yet the flippancy is the most poignant of all—your joshing about your vagrant daily lusts in such an unguarded voice makes them real to me. Having never been to Japan, nor met your wife and child, I've been guilty of picturing it as some rosy, implacable surface, as though by moving from New York to Tokyo and entering a "traditional" Japanese marriage you'd migrated from the complicated world into an elegantly calm piece of eighteenth-century screen art. I'm probably not the first person guilty of finding it convenient to imagine my friends' lives are simpler than my own. It's also possible I began this letter by speaking of A in order to discredit myself as any sort of reasonable counsel, to put you in mind of my abhorrent track record (or maybe I'm just obsessed).

Let me be more honest. I don't spend all that much time imagining Japan. However much you and I speak of our contemporary lives, I picture you as I left you: eighteen years old. You and I were inseparable for the first three years at music and art, then distant in our senior year, then you vanished. Now you're a digital wraith. What would it take to displace the visceral daily knowledge of our teenage years—how extensive would the letters have to be? When I try to think of your marriage I instead tangle, helplessly, in the unexamined questions surrounding our first, lost friendship. I don't mean to suggest *anyone* doesn't find a muddle when they recall that year, launching from twelfth grade to the unknown. But it is usual to have you lucidly before me, daring me, by your good faith in these recent letters, to understand.

Do you remember my obsession with Bess Hersh? Do you remember how you played the go-between? That was junior year, just before the breach between us. Bess was a freshman, a ninth grader. You and I were giddy dorks in rapidly enlarging bodies, hoping that being two years older could stand in, with the younger girls, for the cool we'd never attained. I'll never forget the look on your face when you found me where I waited, at the little park beside the school, and said that Bess's appointed friend, her "second," had confirmed that she *liked me too*.

Bess Hersh saw through me shortly after that. I hadn't known what to do with this coup except bungle it when she and I had a moment alone, bungle it with my self-conscious tittering, my staring, my grin. I tried boy jokes on her, Steve Martin routines, and those don't work on girls in high school. What's required then is some stammering James Dean, with shy eyes cast to pavement. Those shy eyes are what give a girl as young as that breathing room, I think. You mastered those poses in short order—I'd wait until college.

Soon, agonizingly soon, Bess was on Sean Hyman's arm, and I felt that I'd only alerted the hipper Sean to her radiant presence among the new freshmen. But I still cling to that moment when I knew she'd mistaken me for cool, before I opened my mouth, while you were still ferrying messages between us so that she could project what she wished into the outline of me. I still picture her, too, as some sort of teenage sexual ideal, lost forever: her leggy slouching stride, the cinch of worn jeans over that impossible curve from her narrow waist to the scallop of her hips, her slightly too-big nose and fawny eyes. I wonder what kind of woman she grew into, whether I'd glance at her now. Once she gave me boners that nearly caused me to faint. Just typing her name is erotic to me still.

Funny, though, I don't remember speaking to her more than once or twice. I remember speaking with you about her, *chortling* about her, I should say, and scheming, and pining, and once, when we were safely alone in the Sheep's Meadow in Central Park, bellowing her name to the big empty sky. I recall talking this way with you too about Liz Kessel, Margaret Anodyne, and others. I recall the dopey, sexed-up love lyrics we'd write together, never to show to the girls. You and I were just clever enough, and schooled enough in *Mad magazine*, Woody Allen, Talking Heads, Frank Zappa, and Devo, to ironize our sprung lusts, to find the chaos of our new-yearning hearts bitterly funny.

When, six months on, you first began combing your hair differently, and when you began listening to New Romantic bands, and when you began dating Tu-Lin, I was disenchanted with you, M. Violently disenchanted, it seems to me now. I felt all the music you listened to was wrong, a betrayal—you'd quit liking the inane clever stuff, and moved on to music that felt postured and sexy instead. I felt you'd forgotten yourself, and I tried to show you what you'd forgotten. When I'd third around with you and your new Vietnamese girlfriend, I'd seek to remind you of our secret languages, our jokes—if they hadn't worked on Bess they should at least still mean something to you—but those japes now fell flat, and you'd rebuff me, embarrassed.

Of course the worse I fared the harder I tried. For a while. Then that became our falling-out. I must have appeared so angry—this is painful speculation, now. Of course, what seemed so elaborately *cultural* or *aesthetic* to me at the time—I faulted you for hairstyle, music, Tu-Lin's Asianness—all appears simply emotional in retrospect. I was threatened by the fact that you'd gone from pining for girls to having them, sure. But I'd also invested in you all my intimations of what I was about to surrender in myself, by growing up. By investing them in you I could make them something to loathe, rather than fear. Loathing was safer.

Oh, the simple pain of growing up at different speeds!

A page or two ago I supposed I was going to build back from this reminiscence, to some musings on your current quandary, your adult ambivalence about the commitments you entered when you married (I nearly wrote *entered precociously*, but that's only the case by my retarded standard). But I find I'm reeling even deeper into the past. When I was seven or eight, years before you and I had met, my parents befriended a young couple, weirdly named August and Sincerely. I guess those were their hippie names—at least Sincerely's must have been. August was a war resister. My parents had sort of adopted him during his trial, for he'd made the gesture of throwing himself an eighteenth birthday party in the office of his local draft board, a dippy bit of agitprop which got him singled out, two years later, for prosecution. Sincerely was a potter, with a muddy wheel and a red-brick kiln in the backyard of her apartment. She was blond and stolid and unpretentious, the kind of woman who'd impress me now as mannish, a lesbian perhaps, at least as a more plausible candidate for chumming around than for an attraction (I felt she was a woman, then, but she must have been barely twenty, if that).

We'd visit Sincerely often during the six or eight months while August served out his sentence, sit in the yard sipping iced tea she'd poured with clay-stained hands, and in that time I very simply—and articulately, to myself—fell in love. I was still pre-sexual enough to isolate my feelings for Sincerely as romantic and pure. In stories like this one children are supposed to get mixed up, and to imagine that adults will stop and wait for them to grow up, but I wasn't confused for a moment. I understood that my love for Sincerely pertained to the idea of what kind of woman I meant to love in my future life as a man. I promised myself she would be exactly like Sincerely, and that when I met her I would love her perfectly and resolutely, that I would be better to her than I have in fact ever been to anyone—than anyone's ever been to anyone else.

So my love wasn't damaged by August's return from jail (he'd never gone upstate, instead served his whole time in the Brooklyn House of Detention, on Atlantic Avenue). I didn't even bother to resent his possession of Sincerely, which I saw as intrinsically flawed by grown-up sex and diffidence. August wasn't a worthy rival, and so I just went on secretly loving Sincerely with my childish idealism. The moron-genius of my young self felt it knew better than any adult how to love, felt certain it wouldn't blow the chance if it were given one. Not one day I've lived since has satisfied that standard. Of course, it is strange and sad for me now to see a shade of future triangulation in that emotional arrangement—I'd cast August as an early stand-in for R, a man I would pretend was irrelevant even as I fitted myself into his place in life.

What I'd promised to hold on to then, M, is the same thing I'd raged against losing when you began to grow away from me, when I failed the test presented by your sultry new self that senior year. How ashamed that promiser would be to learn—had some malicious time traveler drifted back to whisper it in his ear—about the pointless ruin of my years with A. Those promises we make to ourselves when we are younger, about how we mean to conduct our adult lives, can it be true we break every last one of them? All except for one, I suppose: the promise to judge ourselves by those standards, the promise to remember the child who would be so appalled by compromise, the child who would find jadedness wicked.

Yes, my childish self would read this letter and think me poisoned with knowledge, but the truth is that what I flung against A so recklessly *was* my innocence, preserved in a useless form. The revving heart of my hopefulness, kicked into gear anew, is the most precious thing about me, I refuse to vilify it. I hope I fall in love again. But it's a crude innocence that fails to make the distinctions that might have protected me from A, and A from me. For by imagining I could save her from her marriage, by that blustery optimism by which I concealed from myself my own despair at the cul-de-sac lust had led us into, I forced her to compensate by playing the jaded one on both our behalves. What I mean to say is that I forced her to play me that song, M, by grinning at her like a loon. Like the way I grinned at Bess Hersh. I gave A no choice but to be the dark lady, by being the moron-child who thought love could repair what love had wrecked. A motorcycle that's gone off a cliff isn't repaired by another motorcycle.

Well, I've failed. This whole letter is about A, I see that now. You wonder whether you can stand never to know the touch of a fresh hand, the trembling flavor of a new kiss, and I'm desperately trying to keep from telling you the little I know: it's sweeter than anything, for a moment. For just a moment, there's nothing else. As to all you're weighing it against, your wife and child, I know less than nothing. The wisdom of your ambivalence, the whimsical, faux-jaded wit you share in your letter, as you contemplate the beauties around you, all that poise will be shattered if you act—I can promise you that much. You're more innocent than you know. I speak to you from the dark end of the street, but it's a less informed place than you'd think. All I can do for you is frame the question I've framed for myself: Where to steer the speeding motorcycle of one's own innocence? How to make it a gift instead of a curse?

I think we need a new national anthem.

I'm ending this letter without saying anything about your incredible tale of the salaryman masturbating on the subway. Well, there, I've mentioned it. I'm also grateful to know that Godzilla's not what he's cracked up to be, that he's just another mediocre slugger with a good agent and a memorable nickname. What a joy it would be to see the Yankees really take a pratfall on that move. Bad enough when they pillage the other American teams, but that the world is their oyster too has become unbearable. Of course, the Mets go on signing haggard veterans and I think there's no hope at all, but you can be certain

Giuseppe and I will be out at Shea having our hearts broken this May, as always. In our hearts it's always spring, or 1969, or something like that. I only wish we had some outfielders who could catch the ball.

Yours,

E

This Shape
We're In

IT BEGAN WHEN BALKAN CAME INTO OUR BURROW during cocktail hour and told us he had been in the eye. Earl and Lorna were sitting around sipping gin and tonics and watching me grill a hunk of proteinous rind which I'd marinated pretty nicely and was basting like a real pro and my immediate response was to tell Balkan to go to hell. Marianne offered him a drink and he took it with both hands like it was hot chocolate and went back to boasting about his extraordinary meander and the culture of the forelimbs and the things he'd witnessed peering through the eye: the inky depths of interstellar space (*his* words: *inky depths, interstellar space*). Balkan believed he dwelt in the liver or *seat of the soul* and I happened to know he was wrong, that in fact Balkan and his bunker of weirdos were dwelling in the rump—merely the seat. Balkan was the same age as my son Dennis, was an old pal of Dennis's, in fact. He wouldn't have known the liver from an amphitheater or an orgy and I could be pretty sure he'd been deceived about the eye as well: it wouldn't be the first time some priestly collective mounted a bogus eye and started preaching to deluded seekers and gullible militia types like Balkan about the wonders to be seen, the answers to be had.

But all I said was, "Which eye?"

"Which?"

That's right, kid, I thought, *bring this mystical shit into my burrow and drink up my liquor.* "Right, left, or third?"

"I don't know," said Balkan, hemming. "I just know it was an eye, Mr. F. Don't try to tell me it wasn't." Then: "There's a *third?*"

"Oh yeah," I said. "The visionary eye, looks into the face of God—and God's got his finger in his nostril, to the knuckle. In fact we're a booger, Balkan, hadn't word reached you?" In truth I'd only heard faint legends of a third eye myself—when Dennis was in kindergarten in the pizzle and he came home having played some children's game, chanting under his breath: *Third eye third eye watching me/third eye third eye it can see/third eye third eye set me free/my mother says to pick the very next one!* I yanked Dennis out of that school the next day and that was right about when Marianne and I decided to find our way out to the subburrows. And I knew fuckall about what any such alleged third eye looked out on. Such ignorance is what passed for bliss, those days.

"Don't be mean," said Marianne to me. "I'm sure it was an eye, Balkan, and probably a very important one. You know, we're just not that *interested* in space around here." Her words were a condescending veneer of charm stretched over a yawning gulf of boredom.

Then she asked: "Can I refresh anyone's drink?" It wasn't so much a question as a gesture in the barbecue Kabuki, signaling we should get off the topic and back to some more general jabber along the way to getting potted. There came various murmurs of satisfaction, a bowl of chips was passed around, and Earl asked Balkan a few polite questions about the stripes of rank on his shoulder and what they meant, though I knew he didn't give two hoots on a rusty trumpet.

I slivered off chunks of that marinated rind and put it in buns loaded up with onions and Balkan took one from me and wolfed it like a hunted thing. Poor bastard was malnourished physically and in other ways and I thought for the hundredth time *God Bless marriage, grilling, distilled spirits, and all else that distracts from wayward sons and wayward theories,* and it was while I was in the thick of this coarse, gratifying epiphany, I swear, that Balkan said, "I saw Dennis up there. He's a beggar in the eye."

Marianne, suddenly attentive, said: "What did you say?"

Balkan knew he had her attention now. "Dennis, your

son, sure. He sits in the back of the eye and chants and says prayers for money."

Of course, this was what Balkan had come to say in the first place. It was absolutely like him to *bury the lead*.

"Oh, Balkan, why didn't you bring him back?" said Marianne.

"Don't listen to him," I said to Marianne. "He didn't see *anyone*. Balkan, get screwed." I stood from my chair as though to make a grab or throw a punch, but in fact I still had my drink in my hand, and only lurched.

"Maybe we ought to get going, folks," said Earl, though Lorna was still only halfway through her plate. Lorna nibbled nervously on her sandwich, eyes wide like a ferret.

"He's your son," said Marianne to me. She stepped up and plucked at my glass, which I fought for, causing half my lovely gin to slosh over my wrist and trickle onto my leg and into the astroturf.

"Christ, woman." I said it in my John Wayne voice, a joke which general mush-mouthedness caused to be completely lost if it had stood a snowball's chance in the first place. Still, I thought it pretty good-humored, given the waste of a cocktail.

"Henry," said Marianne. "Dennis needs you. He's your son."

"You ought to listen to Balkan," said Earl, thumping me on the shoulder. "You ought to go with him and bring him back."

"Ha! I ought to send Balkan back with a bill for services rendered. I gave that kid fourteen nonrefundable years of reasonably adequate parenthood, under damned strained conditions. But we'd be assuming Balkan here could even blunder his way back to this so-called eye."

"Right with you, Captain," said Balkan, saluting me.

"Don't call me Captain!" I said. "Don't call me Dad or Captain or capsized or late for dinner!" Okay—so I was engaged in a lot of nervous riffing but nevertheless striking a jocular note, if they could hear it.

They couldn't. Marianne in the relevant particular. She tore off her apron and flung it, straight upwards, where it weirdly hooked on our burrow's fluorescent ceiling fixture. Then she began to cry. "You drove him aw-aw-away—" were the words I heard in the teary, gasping mix.

"Oh, no," protested Balkan, out of his depth. "Dennis isn't *mad* at you and Mr. F—"

"No, he's just turned into a broken, abject beggar," sniffled Marianne. "Dennis couldn't stay mad at a fly—" The oddness of this thought seemed to slow her down, and she left it unfinished.

"It's okay, honey," said Lorna, who was over consoling Marianne with an arm draped around her shoulders in a blink, making me look like a jerk for what I'd been doing instead: fixing another cocktail. I took it to Marianne once it was poured, figuring better late than etc., but paused behind the curtain of the hanging apron to level off the top with a sip which turned out to be half the glass, somewhat damaging my already-thin point. Marianne glared at me, then took it anyway and had a healthy slurp herself. Which seemed to right her ship rather quickly.

"*You go find Dennis and bring him back,*" she said, eyes red and squinky like a mole's, but voice fiberglass-tough.

"No can do," I said. "Dennis is his own, um—" I lost a word here, and aggressively wrong ones pushed forward to take its place: his own *can-of-worms? Commanding officer? Best-case-scenario?* Then in place of any word I substituted a pratfall: losing my balance I grabbed for the apron and tugged down the fluorescent light fixture, bulb shattering against the grill and powdering the remaining cuts of rind with crystalline white dust. The women and Balkan shrieked and danced backwards and Earl, in some sort of sketchy volunteer-fireman impulse, doused the grill and the shattered fixture with his drink. It flared like Baked Alaska, then sizzled greasily and died.

"Wow," I said, gesturing at the strange scene on the grill. "What's for dinner? Looks like smoker's lung!" This came out more aggressive, less self-deprecating than I'd hoped. Balkan scraped at the wreckage on the floor of the burrow with the toe of his boot, and I noticed for the first time that he was wearing a spur. I wondered if he even knew what it was for.

"Get out!" screamed Marianne. "Don't come back without Dennis!"

I reached for Marianne, meaning to hug her into silence but she gripped my arms at the shoulders and so we locked into a stiff tango. "Ur—hey!" We tilted and slid like a lopsided rockinghorse, and Balkan and Lorna scrambled away. Earl had already climbed up into the corridor, and was peering down into our burrow to follow the quote-unquote action.

"Let go of me, you lousy, drunken—" Marianne fished for a word here, came up with: "—clown!" I guess I'd already disqualified or preempted a bunch of other possible insults.

"Well at least I've got a job," I joked, meaning *clown,* but this just wasn't my day for getting punchlines across. I suppose this one was a stretch in the first place, since clown would have been a step up from my current occupation: garbage hider for the subburrow. I basically spent my time sneaking into other parts of the shape—spleen, hind legs, etc.—and concealing our offal and eggshells under other people's shrubbery and mattresses.

Now my feet tangled in the legs of the grill, and Marianne and I went down. "Oh boy," I said. "Feels like maybe I broke something—"

"GET OUT NOW!" screamed Marianne.

"I THINK I WILL!" What a strong hand I had to play.

"YOU DO THAT!"

"HERE I GO AND DON'T COUNT ON ME COMING BACK! I MAY JUST TAKE UP CHANTING MYSELF!"

And so on—the long and the short of it, not that I remember all of the long, is that I found myself with Balkan in the tunnel above the lungs an hour later, having salvaged only the gin jar and my old service revolver before being expelled from the burrow in a hail of Marianne's alternated denunciations and importunings, the former roughly or even precisely deserved, the latter probably useless but driving my secretly fond and guilty heart onward, to quest through parts of the shape I'd wished never to see again in search of a son whose fate a rat's ass meant to me slightly more than. If it matters, I believed I was doing it all for Marianne. I loved Marianne. I never saw her again.

I nudged Balkan awake in the dark of the pew where we were hidden and asked him to pass me the sacramental wine we'd pilfered to follow the gin we'd worn out. Balkan lay sprawled across several knee-pillows, his fingers folded over the drum-tight bulge of his drink-swollen belly where his shirt had hitched up. Before he'd passed out I'd prompted some nice ravings from him concerning the *inky depths*, etc. "The shape is an *intergenerational starship*," he said with immense pride and satisfaction at mastering the five-dollar word and its implications. "We just forgot, that's all. They sent us out to colonize another planet, and we just forgot. Oh, Mr. F, if you saw it you'd know. We've gotta get ready for the landing, I feel it coming, everybody feels it coming—" Now he murmured and handed me the chalice, returned to dozing. But the wine itself was exhausted, down to dregs, like the gin, like Balkan, everyone but me. I couldn't sleep. I was listening to various faint echoes and howls deep in the shape: running feet, some grinding or whirring machine, shouted commands, a distant ringing phone, one-sided moaning. The left lung is a cathedral, one of the largest open spaces in the shape, and noises are transmitted from every side and through every portal. It was a lung that breathed sound, it seemed to me as I huddled there. Balkan's snoring was the metronome for this soundscape's tired rehearsal of options—I didn't want to stay where I was and I didn't want to budge and I couldn't go crawling back to Marianne, not yet anyway. And if Dennis was actually to be found it was plain I would have to be both pilot and navigator, or bush-whacker and safari master, that Balkan was only dead weight and noncomic unrelief. My boy Dennis, and his pal Balkan, the fresh green troops coming to replenish the old—oh boy. *De*generational starship was more like it. I'd had to commandeer Balkan to even get this far, he'd become so utterly turned around within a few paces of my door, hornswoggled by the sameness of the subburrows. That sameness was what I adored, of course, but now I'd been expelled from my kozy korner.

I reviewed my options. Budge it was. It was night-cycle, and easier to travel the spine by dark, I figured. I reached out and twirled the spur on Balkan's ankle, then jerked it sideways sharply. The torque on his foot jerked Balkan out of sleep, too.

"You looked like you were having a nightmare," I lied.

"Uhmmm. Where are we?"

"Out of booze, that's where. And methinks I hear the jingle-jangle of a priest's automatic weaponry. Time to motivate."

"The men will be glad to see you, Captain—"

"You were having a nightmare. C'mon, let's find a bar."

The spine, however, wasn't what it used to be. We staggered out of the cathedral lung and into a revivalist militia roadblock, straight out of Balkan's militant daydreams. It was run out of a storefront I was pretty sure had been the roost of just about my favorite mixologist, back in the Way-Back-When. I didn't want to think about where he might have ended up, old whatsisname, the genius bartender—Highball? Could he have really been named Highball? Anyway, poor Highball's fate or how long it had been since the W.B.W., either one I didn't want to consider. The past is the religion I was raised in, but I don't practice religion.

These camouflage fetishists had two-thirds of the spine's width cordoned off and lit with flares. They searched us and impounded my revolver, then steered me and Balkan into what had been a nice little watering hole, to wait behind a few other hapless stragglers they'd rounded up for interrogation by their "chief officer," a kid barely older than Balkan with a pointy Custer mustache, a wannabe martinet. The only evidence of their HQ's previous incarnation was a shelf of dusty commemorative plates—dead young movie stars and presidents rendered in porcelain—above what had been a shelf full of exotic single malts. "Have you any orders?" he said and I couldn't really keep from saying, "Scotch, rocks." In fact I could see they had put old Highball's fabricator to depressingly pedantic use cranking out some pinkish goo that looked something like Spam, or possibly Oobleck. A couple of guys were eating the stuff out of bowls, while others were using scoops to direct it as it was pumped out and packing it into half-gallon containers like it was ice cream.

"We're headed for the eye, sir," said Balkan, nervously trying to cover my gaffe.

"Why are you calling him *sir?*" I said. "This isn't your, uh, unit, is it Balkan?"

Balkan blinked at me, then spoke to the beady-eyed officer. "Captain Farbur has been away from the field for some time. He asked me to escort him on a tour of recognizance."

I poked Balkan in the ribs. "Don't you mean *reconnaissance?*"

Balkan and the officer both blinked at that one.

"Maybe *pre*cognizance," I said, while I had them going. "We are looking for the *third* eye, right?"

This had an odd effect on the littlest soldier man, as though I'd said *"The password is 'the password'"* or *"These aren't the droids you're looking for."* He grabbed my hand and shook it again, then said in an intimate, confidential tone, "We've been getting some pretty intriguing reports from up around the third eye."

"Ah, *reports*," I said, raising my eyebrow. "From *precognizance?*"

"From various sources," he said defensively. "We've been in touch with Central Command."

"Central Command. Really. Congratulations. Central

Command is not usually so—" I had to search for a deco-
rous word here "—so *forthcoming.*"

"Oh, they've been very *forthcoming,*" boasted the little
soldier, quite relieved that I appeared to credit his break-
through.

"You should see it, Mr. F," said Balkan, blowing our
cover in his excitement, not that it apparently mattered.
"They came through and put in these phones everywhere.
The phones are bright red, that's how you know you've got
a direct channel to Central Command."

"And *they* is exactly—who?" I asked.

The soldier and Balkan looked at one another, each insecure of their own theories about the phones, I guess.

"Central . . . Command?" ventured Balkan at last, as
though I'd be grading his test later.

The soldier nodded eager confirmation. Seemingly that
was what he would have said too, if he'd found his tongue.

"Well, that's exciting," I said, though it wasn't anything
remotely. The echolalic circularity of this exchange was
only going to keep my mind off finding a drink for a very
short time more. "I'm gonna have to get me one a them
bright red phones." I chuckled, and, though plainly bewildered, Balkan and the soldier took the cue and we all had
a good hearty laugh. "Okay, then," I said, taking the soldier's hand again. "We'll report back as soon as we can.
Maybe we'll even call you from Central Command!" More
chuckles. "Hey, you haven't by any chance got a hip flask?"
But now my little soldier's face fell: he wasn't even sure of
the nature of his inadequacy to this request. Should've

known better than to ask of him, or Balkan either, anything in any way *hip*.

Nevertheless, we got my revolver back, a free escort
past their cordon, and a glance at their map, which I was
inclined to trust about as far as it extended into actual
space, say eighteen or twenty inches. Still, I flattered it with
my intense scrutiny. Then I saluted my soldier and he just
about fainted with gratitude. "Come on," I said, giddying-
up Balkan, who wanted to linger and gape at the margin-
ally well-orchestrated maneuvers the Brat Patrol were
conducting on the far side of the spine. "Isn't Don Rondelay's Retreat just off that fork up ahead?"

I actually recognized the spot not thanks to the soldier's
map but due to this being a stretch where for no reason I
could imagine various souls had seen fit over the years to
tie the laces of their old sneakers together and fling the re-
sulting sneaker-bolo upwards so it wound around the high
rafters of the spine, too high for anyone without a hook-
and-ladder to cut them down. There must have been a
hundred pairs of sneakers dangling there. Who knows
how these things get started? But I digress.

"Uh, who?" said Balkan, a little disingenuously, I
thought.

"Come on, Balkan. Don Rondelay's. It's a famous orgy,
longest-running in the whole ribs and shoulders, maybe
the whole shape. Don't say *he's* gone belly-up, you'll break
my heart—" *Belly-up* a mild pun here, since *why not* at an
orgy, right? Wasted on Balkan, needless to say.

"No, it's still there," said Balkan nervously, catching me

by the arm. "I don't see why we ought to—uh, Mr. F,
there's nothing we need from that place—"

"Don't you think we ought to make a report?"

"Oh, no, Mr. F." Very serious now. "I've seen reports.
Activities there are at an, um, complete standstill. I mean,
no one goes in or out anymore—"

"No in or out? *That's* hard to believe." Pathetic, the
shallows of my amusement.

"There's nothing, uh, likely nothing to be learned or
gained or, uh, discerned—"

"Maybe something to be un-learned, though. For the
discerning. That's you and me, Balkan." I tugged out of
his grasp and lurched in the direction my old spider-sense
told me the door to Don Rondelay's Grotto was still to be
found. Balkan hurried after me.

Actually, *standstill* sort of described the situation inside. What I'd remembered as a quite spontaneous and
free-form day-and-night grope-a-thon—sprawled, pulsing, inelegant bodies rich in scars, tattoos and cellulite,
spilled wine, cigarettes stubbed in smeared plates of soft
cheese and onion dip, weird fricative sounds and snorts of
laughter—seemed to have hardened into precious ritual, a
scene as glossy and predictable as silicone. Up front a
buffed "master" in a zipper-mask, leather loincloth, and
hood snapped a whip to direct waxy six-foot women in
G-strings in a series of theatricalized, slow-motion
tableau—coy lesbian scenes, silk-ribbon bondage, lollipop-
sucking, mock-horse-and-rider play—for the benefit of
passive watchers of both sexes. In the second room a

woman in a quasi-military outfit directed a group of young men in a new-recruit fantasy, including strip-searches, buzz haircuts, and light hazing. It was all dimly, tastefully perverted and as remote from a good, crunchy, nutritional orgy as I could fathom. The drill-sergeant woman spotted something in Balkan the minute we walked in, crooked her finger at him, and he fell in place with her other recruits, bugging his eyes at me helplessly. I waved dismissively—*knock yourself out!*—and pressed through to the next room, certain there had to be a bar somewhere, or at least a concession stand.

The inner sanctum was the most ludicrous of all. Lit by strobe a group of women writhed and danced while men seated at a long glass counter watched not the bodies but their shadows reflected on the far wall. The place was perfumed and soundtracked like a mausoleum. Old Don Rondelay himself presided, the fat corrupt toad—I was oddly pleased to see him leaning there in the back doorway smoking a stogie and surely counting real and imaginary gold behind his half-lidded eyes. The more things change, etc. And tending bar at the counter was none other than Highball.

He quit polishing a shaker long enough to salute me. "Long time no see."

I mimed crawling out of the desert to an oasis, choked at my neck to stress the urgency of my thirst.

He poured a shot onto rocks, kept pouring until it was two shots. "This still your usual?"

"Not usual enough."

"What brings you around?"

"Fight with the wife." I slugged at his—well, Don Rondelay's—good bourbon, savored the heat of it.

"Wanna talk about it?"

"What's to talk about? It's the typical stuff: son's no good, third eye might hold secret of the universe but conversely might not, man's gotta do what a man's gotta do—"

"I more than understand."

I raised my glass to him. "Is it just me, or is this place a little on the, uh, formal and regimented side all of a sudden?"

"Tell me about it."

"This militia craze that's sweeping The Young People of the Shape Today knows no bounds."

"Martial memory," agreed Highball.

"What the fuck is *that* supposed to mean?" I said, surprised by the ragged claw of anger that went scuttling across the floor of my gut. "I mean, memory of *what*?" Or had he said *Marshall Memory*—like a hero in a Western?

He held up both his hands. "I just work here."

"Mr. F, Mr. F—" It was Balkan. He came in to the bar area bare-chested, clutching his shirt in one hand and his unfastened belt in the other, running like a kid who'd screwed up at potty.

"Hello, Balkan."

He buckled his belt and straightened up, saluted me with the free hand. "Mr. F, they've got one of those red phones I was telling you about, a line to Central Command—"

"Well hey ho," I said. "Guess we ought to check it out."
I drained my glass, plunked it in front of Highball. "What
do I owe you?"

Highball just raised his chin at Don Rondelay, who nodded back and lifted his cigar to me. "You're good here,"
said Highball. "Don't be a stranger."

The red phone was mounted in a cubby off the second
room. It was in use. Another guy about Balkan's age was
curled around it with his back to us, speaking in a low,
gummy voice. "Yeah, that's it," he said. "God, you sound
so good, I wish I could see you right now. You know what
I'd do if we were in the *same room* right now?" His hand,
I noticed at this point, was jammed into his pants. The guy
was having better fun than the actual patrons of the orgy,
far as I could tell. Balkan stood staring dumbly, tugging
his shirt back into place, waiting for me to decode his
world for him yet again.

"I think this particular red phone has been corrupted,"
I told Balkan. "Must be something about the milieu. Context wins as usual."

"Maybe we ought to, you know, seize control of the
phone," he said weakly.

"Too soon for any sort of seizure," I told him. "We're
still in fly-in-the-ointment mode here, gathering info. *Recognizance,* remember?"

"Ointment?"

"It's where flies go when they're sick of the wall," I said.
"C'mon, I think I know where we can get another dose."

• • •

Navigating by the compass of our bender, Balkan and I made our way through the upper chest, honoring as many of my old haunts as still stood, otherwise cadging booze from sentries running nutrient fabricators on behalf of a variety of local despots, tinhorn regional sheriffs and faintly charismatic cult figureheads. Everywhere troops of one definition or another were massing, being drummed into this or that obscure warlike fervor, whether under the guise of religious or scientific or merely paranoiac revelations provided by up-to-the-minute reports and rumors from the various competing eyes. We ducked conscription, needless to say. No credit to Balkan, but we ducked. Our bender petered just as we found our way into the neck, and it was there we finally crashed for a bout of R&R at a flop run by missionaries of the nuclear-shelter-theory persuasion. *"We must strive to comport ourselves in a manner befitting the privileged survivors of worldwide catastrophe,"* was the texture of hairshirt they were selling at the interminable lectures we and fifteen or so other stragglers had to sit through just to get a free bowl of their lousy cream of nothing soup. *"We owe this to the many millions who perished when we alone were granted salvation in the shelter of the shape. Those perished and their countless generations of children who will never be. We live for them and we must live as they would have had us live,"* never imagining of course that the countless unborn billions might have enjoyed a snort of hooch now and again.

They were pushing something on the order of a twelve-step program for the spirit within and the shape without, and we put up with their ranting and blather for as long as it took to get a couple of squares and a ten-hour snooze on their narrow cots.

It was as I ground the nuggets of sleep out of the corners of my eyes and began to anticipate scaring up a hair of the dog that I found the eldest and most bearded and sanctimonious of those long-robed propagandists waiting by the side of my cot.

"May I ask you a question, sir?"

"You already have."

"In these great times, sir, it is a shame and a sorrow to see a man of your stature and accomplishment leading a band of two on so paltry a mission as that which brought you to our door."

"True, it's barely more than a paltry-raid," I agreed.

He didn't acknowledge the pun. "In these great times of ours a man of your particular rank, sir, should lead a sizable and righteous legion. The shape is much in need of the leadership you could provide."

"Could would should," I said. "Maybe I've got a higher calling, a family duty. Blood being thicker than hoo-ha."

"Family values are not incompatible with our views, sir."

I noticed now that Balkan was gone from his cot, along with the others who'd slept in our room. The goofballs had arranged for this to be a private confab. "Make your point," I said.

"The surface temperature is cooling, Geiger readings indicate a readiness for human reoccupation. This will be a task for the greatest among us—despite how they may have consoled or distracted themselves through the years of waiting for that which we all must desire—"

"Yah? yah, what Geiger counter, whose readings?"

"Before we share our secrets, sir, we need a sign of good faith from you. In our circle there are those—though I am not among them—who fear you already represent some other faction, that you feign your inconstant ways and are with us now on some mission of infiltration."

"Hey, far be it from me to *feign*." I winced at myself. The guy would have me babbling pentameter any minute now. "Why don't you just spill it? If I don't get with your program I promise to drown your precious secrets along with the rest of the stuff I'm pickling."

He lowered his voice to a biblical *basso profundo*. "Let us show you our eye."

I whistled. "Boy, you're some heavy dudes. Just a local outfit working the gutter patrol, that's what I took you for. Deep *in mufti,* I guess. Your own eye, wow. That a right or a left eye?"

"It is the *one true eye,* sir."

"And it's yours."

"We have exclusive rights, yes sir."

"And you think so damn much of me—wow."

"Would you come with us, sir." Another of the elders stepped out of the corridor, and I saw them trade nods.

"My man Balkan is coming along, isn't he?"

"We would prefer you visit alone. Your companion is busy playing video games at the moment, sir, and I doubt he'll notice your absence."

They had it all figured, a bit too neat for me. "Tell you what," I said. I slid my feet into my shoes, which were permanently knotted, and stuck my revolver back into my belt. "I'll look at your eye on one condition. Your bunch has got its sanctimonious grip on a fabricator, probably more than one, right? I want a quart container of Old Overholt to oil my aching wheels and levers, something with a cap or screwtop so I can take it on the yellow brick road, then we'll be off to see the wizard. And no temperance lectures, please—you want the warhorse, you fill his feedbag."

"I'm sorry, sir—Old Overholt?"

"Just tell it to the fabricator. It'll remember."

So I went, after breakfasting deeply on the whisky just to get their back hair up and chase a measure of the static from my forebrain. The two elders flanked me, solemn as dried fruit. On our way upstairs to their ultra-secret eye we passed another of the red phones. It was mounted in an Olde-London style booth and just for kicks I pried open the door as we passed so I could hear what the guy using the phone was on about. He was dressed in gray-green fatigues but the inflamed look on his face was pretty civilian.

"Can you feel it?" he chanted into the red phone. "Can you take it all? It's filling you up—"

I raised an eyebrow at my escorts, but nobody said anything.

It turned out that what the elder had meant by "exclusive rights" was that he and his soup-kitchen boys had struck a deal—likely for food, protection, who knew what else—with a clique of young nuns who controlled the eye. And I do mean controlled. The first met us in a small antechamber, the entrance of which had been masked by a large and stinking garbage dumpster. She wore a heavy ring of keys on a chain around her waist and a thick black cape and cowl, but when she turned her head I could see she wasn't more than eighteen or twenty, with bright red cheeks, a dewy chin. And the cheeks were active, jawing, working at something: I thought at first some sort of speaking-in-tongues subvocalizing, then realized—bubble gum. She keyed open the door at the rear of the chamber and we entered a long, desolate corridor, lit with candles, where two more nuns—one for each of us now, I tried not to shame myself by thinking—waited silently. The corridor was hot and nearly airless, the smell of garbage overwhelming, and I wondered if the nun's zone had suffered some breakdown of atmosphere processing, coolant leakage, maybe a complete loss of power. It would explain the candles, and the nuns' dependence on the dopes from downstairs. Plus air this dead and hot wasn't something women in woolly cowls likely suffered solely for aesthetic or ascetic purposes. On the whole, I thought, an unpromising spot for an ontology-shattering eye. But maybe I'd find temporary employment with the nuns as a garbage hider—my only true calling, after all. They sure could use one.

There was a bit more rigmarole and a whole bunch

more nuns, a majority of them also chewing gum under their cowls, before we were shown into an equally muggy circular chamber, lit again with candles, the ceiling studded with hundreds of tiny reflective stickers in the shapes of stars and moons and ringed planets, that old headshop dorm-room staple. The chamber's stepped tile floor inclined towards a thirty-foot-high black curtain, which veiled the furthest section of curved wall: presumably the you-guessed-it. When the curtain was parted I took another slug of Old Overholt, thought *an ice cube, my kingdom for an ice cube,* and stepped up for a look.

It was pretty impressive. A shoreline horizon stretched out, sand and ocean, distant jetty of rocks, and the shock, the vaulting endless shock of sky. And right in the center of the frame—for it was a frame, most artfully composed—a vast figurative sculpture, a titan in rotting green copper, jutted at an impossible angle from its place half-swallowed in the sand. The figure was a totem of a woman in a robe and a spiked headdress. She bore a torch to heaven, only it was now tipped away to point at the edge of sky and water instead. Seabirds wheeled and clouds tumbled ever so slightly in the sky, but this panorama was a tape loop or I was a monkey's commanding officer. The nuns were sure to draw the curtain before much longer. I didn't give them the chance.

"Boys, you've been rooked," I said.

The nuns at either end of the curtain only bowed their heads. The elders who'd brought me here stepped closer, and the three of us, all sweating like pigs, peered through

the eye at the epic scene. It was a thing of beauty, really, if
you took it for what it was: installation art. I wondered
what genius was behind the fallen grandeur of that statue
in the sand—it somehow didn't seem the handiwork of an
eighteen-year-old nun. I could imagine if I let myself that
the statue was another shape, that it too was jammed full
of people wondering if they were alone and that we were
lodged in the sand of the same beach just a few hundred
yards away. That perhaps Balkan was half-right, we were
an intergenerational starship, one of a vast fleet, only not
in space at all. We'd long-ago landed on this beach and
merely didn't have the sense to open the airlock and look
around. The statue was dignified and stupid—its upright-
ness didn't matter in the least, not tilted sideways as it was.
It made me think of me and Marianne, us trying to raise
a kid in the subburrows as though life in the shape could
make sense, as though we could raise a torch to the sky,
and instead having it go all to hell. It also nagged at me,
that image, seemed something I should but didn't want to
remember, the name of the statue, the movie the still was
from. And that in turn reminded me of the fact itself that
there were *things I didn't wish to remember.* Whichever
way I contemplated it the statue image was dire and sad
and made me feel the poison of years in my aching bones
and I stood and lost myself in it for a moment, nursing the
whiskey, feeling sorry for myself and the poor credulous
missionaries who'd come to worship this balderdash.

"Fleeced, by a flock of nuns," I said. "And you probably
ought to be *de*frocked, for that matter. I mean, come now,

gentlemen. You can even see the pixels." I mopped the sweat off my neck with my sleeve, and turned my back on the eye.

"The cynic sees only what the cynic allows himself to see," said the first elder, he of the bedside ministrations.

"Whatever. We're barely halfway up the neck in the first place. This couldn't be an eye, no matter what movie was playing. It's more along the lines of a *tracheotomy*." I offered the bottle around, figuring they could use it about now. No takers. "All right, ladies, get us out of here. But first permit me to use your john, if you would."

"I like that, oh yeah, so I tell you to do it faster, and you do it faster, and I like it faster, but then you tell me to go slow, you don't want to come yet, so I do go slow—"

The red phone in the spiral staircase was occupied too. "Awful lot of people having *phone sex* with Central Command these days," I said to Balkan, just jerking his chain.

He'd been in a lousy mood ever since I pulled him out of the rec room and told him what he'd missed, the nun-tended eye, the lady in the sand. I made up some shit too, about how I'd pulled my revolver and blasted a hole in the screen they were claiming as a vista, and how the *inky, airless depths of interstellar space* came whooshing in and sucked away all the oxygen and gravity so we were bouncing around like human motes and one of the missionaries flew through the hole in the screen and I had to rescue a bunch of the screaming nuns single-handedly—Balkan would swallow just about anything, and he was, under-standably, a bit miffed to have spent the whole time play-ing *Frogger.* He didn't say anything and we continued up the spiral stairs until the moans of the soldier on the red phone were out of earshot.

Balkan knew his way back after all, to the eye in question. *Left eye,* I believe it was in retrospect, though I got a bit turned around myself, and blacked out for a spell in the jaw and nose. I remember something about pulling Balkan out of a bar fight and it wasn't Balkan, it was some other guy instead and he was about to sock me when I pulled my rusty trusty revolver and then Balkan came out and we ran—something about that. What's less deeply shrouded in mental fog is the Buddhist commune in the bridge of the nose where they fed and bathed and reclothed us—I'd pissed my pants at some point, the shame centering in not being able to say exactly when or how long I'd been going around like that. For a religious order the Buddhists were pleasantly free with their rice wine and so we got a nice re-launch though we were dressed now in saffron robes and our heads were shaved. But shortly thereafter Balkan ran into some brethren from his own militia—the rump boys, or "liver" gang, as they preferred to believe—and we ex-changed our robes for militia garb. Balkan got his corpo-ral's stripes back, and they fitted me in a Napoleonic jacket with epaulets and felt buttons. I looked like Marlon Brando in *Mutiny on the Apocalypse Now.*

We'd just drained our last bottle of the monk's sake when we rounded a corner and found it. The line to get in for a glimpse of Balkan's favored eye stretched down a vast corridor towards the cheek, too long to see the head of the line from the end, and there were people camped out who'd plainly been there for weeks, playing chess, sleeping on cardboard boxes, changing diapers on squalling infants, taking turns on a red phone. Concessionaires, missionaries, recruiters and soapbox propagandists were working the crowd, selling cigarettes, transcendence, death-by-glory and other ideologies.

"Did you wait on this when you got in before?" I asked Balkan.

"It—it moves quicker than it looks," he said with embarrassment.

"Holy hell," I said. "That's harshing my mellow, big-time." The closer we got to finding Dennis the more looped I needed to be. I was at a nice pitch right at that moment and shacking up with the squatters was out of the question. "Let's go." I pushed up through the crowd milling at the end of the line and started for the front. Balkan followed, as we snaked along the line drawing stares and jeers and come-ons of a few different flavors. We found, surprise surprise, a pair of young soldiers manning the door at the top of the line.

"Where's Dennis?" I whispered to Balkan.

"Inside," he said. "You'll see."

"Alrighty then." I inhaled deeply and drew out of myself a deep-chested command-baritone. Albeit aloft on drunkard's breath. "Private, seal this door behind us. We're going in."

The soldiers widened their eyes, but stood firm.

Balkan showed mettle for once. "Do you understand who you're talking to?" he demanded, poking a finger into one sentry's chest.

"Sir, yes sir!"

"Good, then. So let's get with the program."

"Now just *wait one minute there, buster.*" This from behind us, a woman's voice. At the head of the line, a young couple dressed in hippie paisley and with identical greasy bangs, him sheepish, projecting desperate hopes of non-involvement, she fiery with indignation. "We've been waiting here for *three days,* along with a whole lot of other people. Who says you can just barrel up here and skip the line?"

"It's a—military matter," I said weakly, hating to hear myself begin playing that particular card with a civilian. The militia boys got a thrill out of it, I knew, but I didn't really like the way it made me feel inside.

"Who *cares?*" said the hippie chick. "We *all* want to see the eye. We all have our *very important* reasons."

"Military-important is different from regular-important," whined Balkan, his moment of gravitas passed.

"Fuck this," I said, feeling suddenly impatient and criminal, not really into procedure *at all.* I whipped out my revolver, hoped she couldn't spot at close range the frozen-with-rust trigger under my finger.

Whether for that reason or some other, she wasn't impressed. She pulled a half-wilted daisy out of her hair and slipped it neatly into the barrel, where it drooped impotently. We all stood in a semi-circle around this astonishment of a woman and stared at the limp flower in dumb silence. Her boyfriend looked like he wanted to tackle her to the ground himself.

One of the sentries took a leaf from Balkan's book and pointed a finger at her. "DO YOU KNOW WHO YOU'RE DEALING WITH, YOUNG LADY?" He being, just incidentally, as young as the girl, or younger.

"Of course," she said. "Everybody knows who he is. He's a garbage hider who used to be important, but he isn't anymore. Why don't you go back to your little bowel in the subbowels, garbage hider, and leave the rest of us alone?"

"Please, let's not get gratuitously ugly," I said. "That's *burrow* in the *subburrows*." This being among the more important euphemisms in my existence, and I'm sure I don't have to explain why.

A nascent hubbub began rippling back through the line behind the couple, and I knew it was time to cut this short. "C'mon, Balkan." I turned to the girl one last time. "Age before beauty, baby. We won't be long."

The proscenium was a little more persuasive this time, a tad more on the scale of one of the shape's original, actual eyes: a planetarium-sized oak-lined hall with a series of recessed conference tables and a waist-high polished brass rail running along the front of the eye's opening. The room was lit gently by green-shaded desk lamps on the tables in the rear. Three tourists stood at the rail gazing into the depths silently—all I could see from here was blackness, possibly inky but I couldn't say yet for sure—but from the back of the room, in the conference area, I heard a murmur of prayer or discussion which echoed majestically across the vaulted ceiling. If it wasn't a true eye it was a copy with a lot of integrity, that much was sure. It stirred something in me, some faint lost sense of grandeur or stature, an impulse to assert my place in the shape with pride, rather than to huddle and cope in some marginal, contemptible organ.

"Where's Dennis?" I whispered again.

Balkan nodded in the direction of the conference tables, the murmurs.

I found him sitting cross-legged on one of the inlaid-wood tables, with a bowl of coins in front of him, chanting lightly, his eyes rolled back, slits of lid showing only white.

"Dennis?"

"Dad?" He jerked to attention, saintly posture abandoned.

"Yeah, kid, it's me." I reached out, but an impulse to clap him sharply on the ear became tender in mid-air, and I riffled his lopsided haircut instead.

"Wow." He looked, saw Balkan, scoped the room to be sure, I suppose, that we weren't spearheading some invasion of troops into his holy chamber. "They said you were coming, that you'd been seen marching around."

"Who said?"

"Lots of people. You lost all your hair?"

"Shaved."

"Wow. I guess you're gearing up for a really major operation, huh?"

"I don't know about that, son. My head was shaved by some Buddhists."

"Oh." I could see that one didn't exactly compute, but he let it go. Probably thought it was classified information, a code-word or some such. "So have you looked at the eye, dad? It's so beautiful."

"It looks beautiful, son. I'd like to go have a closer look."

"You should. Then, I don't know—you and Balkan want to go get something to eat or something?" He was so humble and unrebellious I wanted to weep. I would rather he threw his idiot philosophy in my face, just for the display of backbone. Instead he was an amiable noodle.

All I said was: "Sounds great, Dennis."

I nodded at Balkan. He stayed with Dennis and I went to the rail.

Black, absolute. That's what I saw at first, and so I leaned in closer to the glass, expecting something more. There was nothing more. It was seamless, glintless, fearless, indifferent black—no stars. The curve of the glass cornea reflected the faint light, the green lampshades and oak-paneled tones of the room behind me, my own wondering expression, gin-blistered nose, gleaming pate. The black on the other side of the glass was either infinitely flat or infinitely deep. There was no point of reference, no glimmer or ripple or scratch in the black to give a cue either way. It might have been the bottom of the ocean floor, and on the other side of the glass a million pounds of pressurized water waiting to flood the shape and drown us and return us to our primordial origins. It might have been the vast pupil of God's or Big Brother's unblinking eye. It might have been a vidscreen turned off. Just about the only thing it couldn't have been was the inky depths of interstellar space, because last I checked stellar involved stars.

Dennis didn't balk at leaving with us. Seeing them walk ahead of me, Balkan in his ill-fitting uniform and Dennis padding along in bare feet, the two of them talking about whatever, I remembered Dennis and Balkan playing together as eight or nine year-olds and it just about broke my heart, thinking of their innocence then and, really, still. Their impressionable hearts might now be all invested in grim, cryptic yearnings, in strained, over-serious postures— yet it was innocence nevertheless, innocence all the more so. I wanted nothing worse at that moment than never to see boys stripped of their boyishness, never to see them led into battle as I myself had once been led. Never to see it. And never to lead.

"I'd like to help you find the third eye, Dad," said Dennis humbly when we got away from the maelstrom of that corridor, the sorry population waiting in line to stare into the utterly black eye, waiting to prop up whatever screwed-up hope or lousy, third-hand theory had brought them there in the first place.

"We'll see, Dennis." I was fantasizing about a vodka gimlet at that moment, actually, and my silly brain was thinking *gimlet-eyed, maybe find a gimlet in the eye*—"If there even is one, which I'm still not persuaded—"

That, as it happened, was when Balkan snapped. We were strolling past a soldier on a red phone, just another kid of course, but he was saying something like "So my tongue is licking the line between your navel—" and Balkan ripped the receiver from his grasp and knocked the kid onto the floor.

"Hello? Hello? Is this Central Command?" Balkan's eyes were wild with the release of long-deferred frustration. "IS THIS CENTRAL COMMAND?"

The kid got up out of the dust of the floor, his lower lip sticking out, his expression all pouty at being bullied away from the phone, hand still in his pants. "Vamoose," I told him. "Scram. Here—" I held out my hand to Balkan. "Gimme."

"Okay, Mr. F. They're not saying anything. I don't understand."

I took the receiver. "Hello?" I said. There was silence, then a crabbed, squawking voice said "Hello?"

"Is this, uh, Central Command?"

"Ceeentraaal Commaaaand," screeched the voice. "Do me, baby."

"I'm sorry?"

"*Oh* yeah," said Central Command. "*That's* it. That's it. *That's it, that's it!*"

I figured: what the hell. "So, is there a third eye?"

"Touch my third eye! That's it, baby! Oh yeah! Aaaawwk!" This last was less than persuasively orgasmic, more a strangled bleat.

Irked, I hung up the phone, then shrugged helplessly at Balkan. "Central Command is, uh, out of order." Balkan furrowed his brow.

"Dad?" Dennis had been watching our little skit with calm detachment, his head cocked ever so slightly, like a puppy's.

"Yes?"

"When I said I wanted to help you find the third eye—?" Dennis had somewhere developed that excruciating habit of finishing ordinary statements with an insecure tone of questioning, as though he'd spent his childhood having the word *NO!* bellowed at him. Which emphatically wasn't the case. I'd raised that kid like I was running an egg-and-spoon race through a minefield, and he was the egg.

"Yes?"

"I *meant* I might really be able to help you find it."

Two operatives had sought Dennis out at his place in the eye, and after giving him alms for a few chants—"I did a really good one with the syllables *UR* and *OW*" was his memorable digression—told him they wanted to talk. They said they knew he was interested in the question of the third eye, though how they'd come by this information Dennis couldn't explain. They imparted to him an understanding of how the body/brain barrier was pretty much impermeable, *with one exception,* and then explained that they wished to entrust him with coordinates of this crucial exception, the reason being that another operative would be coming by, a fellow who would need to be told how to *permeate the impermeable,* in order to make a top-secret visit to the shape's brain, which was where the third eye was hidden—atop the brain. They wished for Dennis to function as their contact, hiding in plain sight as he already was (in the form of a contemptible, hebephrenic beggar). These operatives, whom Dennis, when asked to characterize them, declared *"actually really nice guys,"* displaying an impoverishment of both self-protective instincts and descriptive powers that left his dear father appalled, led him bodily from the eye to the place where we now stood, he and I and Balkan, in front of a hole-in-the-wall restaurant in the upper nose called *Not Burn Down.* The smell coming out of *Not Burn Down* suggested the name was either abject plea or foolhardy provocation.

The specialty of the house was *rind with curd,* but their gimmick was this: the rind had been formed into the shapes of various animals, then hung from giant meathooks in a gruesome line along the front of the grill. The animals were all out of scale, the pig and duck and lamb and cow and ostrich the same size, but there was one incongruous showpiece, a large horse. Well, not larger than a *real horse,* considerably smaller in fact, but in the cramped space of the storefront and by comparison to the other rind-creatures it loomed. The grillmaster stood behind the fuming, sputtering fire and slivered chunks off the animals showily, with a long curved knife and what appeared to be a miniature Satan's pitchfork. TRY ARE MIXXE GRILLE! shouted a smoke-stained banner on the far wall, and the few disconsolate customers all seemed to be doing that, their plates heaped with various chunks of blackened rind and sides of curd—though from appearances the pig-shaped-rind and the horse-shaped-rind and all the rest were the same proteinous gluten through and through.

"This way," whispered Dennis, and he led us to the back of the restaurant, towards the door to a darkened back room. The grillmaster stepped up and barred the way, brandishing his knife and skewer in an X across his chest to suggest the possibility of some foul, utensil-based martial art.

Hothead that I am—or possibly the smell was getting to me—I pulled my revolver. "Out of the way, or your animals get it," I growled, putting my gun's muzzle to the rind-horse's ear.

"No, no, High Commander," said the grillmaster, bowing deeply. "I could never stand in your way. I merely wished to say it is a great honor to have you come here. We have all waited for this day with hope and trembling." He finished the bow with a flourish, and like a toreador waved his skewer to indicate our way past him. "Please, sir."

Shamed into silence, I lowered my weapon, and we went inside.

The dumbwaiter was barely big enough for the three of us. Balkan sat in my lap, and Dennis's elbow lodged in my ear. The grillmaster waved us farewell, closed the tiny door, and flipped the lever that propelled us upwards. Crammed into the dark little cubicle with Balkan and Dennis I fantasized we were being injected into the shape's brain, and I wondered then if we were a depressant or a euphoric, a virus or a cure. I was, in other words, beginning to entertain that we were *something,* that our homely little band was, however uncanny, a more-than-negligible force or irritant within the shape.

"Mr. F?"

"Yes, Balkan."

"You're a good man, Mr. F. I just wanted to say that."

"Thank you, Balkan."

We thumped to a stop at the top of its shaft and tumbled out, like circus clowns from a little import. We'd outletted in an empty corridor, one chilly and clean and almost blindingly brightly lit. We were surrounded by a tightly wound team of shock troops even as we were uncrimping our joints, rubbing our eyes, and smoothing our rumpled uniforms—hearing the click of an automatic safety lifting I looked up to find four of them kneeling with us in their sights while another four came hurtling and grunting—"Go, go, go, go!"—around a corner, smoothly unholstering as they fell in behind the others. I had to admire their real polish and precision—these were something more than the fantasizing househusbands and weekend reservists roaming the bulk of the shape lately. They knew how to stay out of one another's lines of fire, a rarer distinction than you'd think. Balkan tumbled into an elaborate pose of surrender, elbows-to-knees, head ducked, fingers laced behind his neck, so efficiently I wondered if he'd been rehearsing it. Dennis opened his hands like Al Jolson singing "Mammy" and began to chant, "Ah, da, ma, aaah, daaah, maaah." Oh, what a goose he was. Me, I chucked my rusty firearm so it slid spinning on the tile to a place at the toe of the team captain's boot.

"We come in pieces," I said, nodding to include my idiot company. "All marbles not necessarily included."

"Up!" said the team leader, waving his piece at Balkan and Dennis, who was kowtowing as he keened.

"Is *that* how we got here?" I smacked my forehead in mock disbelief. But Mr. Severity wasn't going to get baited into a lot of curlicued patter. Having proved his verbal chops with a single syllable, he and his troop made do with pantomime thereafter, wedging their firearms into our backs and force-marching us in single file down the corridor in the direction from which they'd come.

I was separated from Balkan and Dennis at the half-open door of an executive office, the last in a long series of offices we'd passed. Balkan and Dennis were hustled away with the majority of the troops, and I was nudged inside.

"Farbur, is that *you?*"

I squinted at the man behind the desk, not fully believing my eyes. He wore the same dapper uniform as his troops, but nothing could cover the roguish, insouciant expression, or the drunkard's blossoming veins that networked his cheeks and nose.

"Peabody? *Dutton* Peabody?"

"Well, well. Have a seat, Farbur. *Take a load off.* Boys,

feast your eyes on none other than Henry Farbur. I've been waiting a long time for this day!"

"I thought you were a *newspaperman*, Peabody. In the left hind shank, if memory serves." It *didn't,* but hey. "How'd you end up in command up here?" Somewhere back behind the misty veils of time, Dutton Peabody had run a fairly good tabloid on mimeograph paper, called *The Shinbone Star.* Daily sheet—good crime blotter, lively personals section, editorials yellow only in ways I approved.

"Times change, old solder. Times change and men adapt."

I couldn't disagree. "Too bad it's not the other way around, though, isn't it?"

"You may have a point there, Farbur. You may well have a point. Boys, let me have a word with Mr. Farbur here alone, if you would." Of course he drew a nice bottle of amber stuff out of his desk before his troopers had even shut the door.

"To—service."

I drank to his toast, dimly ashamed at the implicit comparison between his crisp uniform and crack troops and my goonish costume, my slapstick stooges. The liquid fire went down good, though, chasing away meemies of various kinds, the eerie fateful echoes that had been building up around me in the past days. It was high time to shake them off. If an old joker like Peabody could thrive in this sober atmosphere of obligation and rearmament, then I ought to be able to wiggle through, just as long as I kept nicely oiled. I drained the glass.

"This is just what the doctor ordered," I joshed. "And the distracter, and the defector, and the disjointer. They all ordered the same thing."

"You sound like a man with something on his chest." He poured me another.

"Oh, for a little while there I was afraid I'd lost sight of the objective—that being: *to lose sight of the objective.* But here's the antidote." I hoisted the glass, winked broadly, slurped away a mouthful.

"If I follow you, it sounds like there might actually be two objectives."

"Yup, that's one way to look at it. Two objectives: Preparedness and, uh, its opposite. One-hundred-percent vigilant wakeful readiness is our first priority. Second priority: blissful, slumbering-idiot complacency." I was giddy with my own wit, drunk on it as much as on the scotch. *Oh, self-love and self-involvement, sweet priceless obfuscators of grim reality!*

As if reading my mind, Peabody said, "First objective, deception, second objective, self-deception."

"Deception?" I played possum. "I don't know from *deception.* Who were we trying to deceive?" I knocked back the rest of the shot. "Man, that's killer shit."

"You're like the guy in the joke, Henry. You forgot what you drink to forget."

"On the good days I forget. I was having a bad one just now."

He lowered his voice. "Your bad day isn't over, General Farbur." I looked up from my glass and caught him staring. Peabody and I ought to have been two old salts knocking a few back, getting three sheets to the thin wind coming out of the air ducts. But now I noticed his own drink was untouched.

Don't drag me back, I wanted to warn him. Instead I said, "I resigned my commission. I'm nobody's general, haven't been for twenty-odd years. I'm a garbage hider."

"You really need to take a look at the eye, Henry." Now he drank.

Peabody and I stepped back out into the brightly lit corridor, into an atmosphere of muted pomp. A dozen of his troopers were lined up at attention along the wall, and Balkan and Dennis stood with them. They'd each been issued clean uniforms and they looked, I had to admit, pretty dapper, pretty upright. Things were changing, wheels were turning, whether I chose to acknowledge them or not. Peabody stepped up to Balkan and Dennis and patted them each lightly on the cheek, and they stood inert and proud, eyes fixed on some middle distance, some imaginary battle, waiting to be told to be at ease. Dennis was tall in his new boots.

"They're going to make great soldiers, Henry," said Peabody. "We'll train them in, start while you're upstairs. In no time they'll be damn fine fighting men."

"Dennis?" I said.

"Sir? I mean, Dad?"

"Is this what you want?"

"Uh, yes Dad sir."

Now I wished to hear him chant again, hear him boast of the nirvana of intoned syllables. Yes-Dad-sir would do fine, I thought: yesdadsir, yesdadsir. I wanted to hear it and throw a coin in his cup myself. I wanted to see him in bare feet, scuttling dorkishly. I thought of Marianne, how she'd commanded me to *bring him back.*

"All right, kid. We'll—we'll talk about it when I get back."

Peabody dismissed the unit and they marched away. I let myself be led across the corridor, to a locked stairwell door. Peabody keyed it open, then pressed the key into my palm. Like the floor of offices, the stairwell was clean and spare and flooded with light. There wasn't a trace of human life, not a whiff, not an echo.

"We'll be waiting to hear from you, Henry," said Peabody, clapping my shoulder.

"Okeydokey," I said in a moron voice. I wished feebly to defuse the air of immanence, of severity. But *okeydokey* didn't make any impression on Peabody at all.

"These men are positively aching for your command. You only have to say the word."

I was at a loss.

"Hey, almost forgot—here." Peabody reached into his interior breast pocket, emerged with a slim hip flask, in filigreed silver. I dimly recognized the elaborately decorated monogram: H-A-F. Henry Allan Farbur. I lifted it out of his hands. It sloshed promisingly.

"I've been saving it for you. Smell."

I took a sniff. It was good stuff, very good stuff.

"We know how you work, Henry. I don't have to say any more, do I? Welcome back."

I screwed the cap back, my fingers savoring the neatly worked metal, the elegance of the flask. I slipped it into the pocket of my Napoleon jacket.

"I—I think I'll go see the eye now, Dutton."

"You do that." He winked. "We're not going anywhere without you."

At the top of the stairwell was another locked door. It took the key Peabody had slipped me.

There were thirty of the birds—I counted. Large white parrots, football-sized, with a plume of feathers at the neck. *Thick-billed parrots*—I was fairly certain of the breed name. The birds stood on mounts in cubicles in the vast white office, each wearing a headset with a vocal mic curved to meet the front of its bill. A spiral cord trailed from each headset to a phone on the cubicle desks, which were otherwise clean, though the cubicle floors were heaped with little white-green pyramids of birdshit. The odor in the room was thin and intense, like ammonia, and the sounds the parrots made formed a cacophonous squalling wall-of-sound:

"Put it in there! Put it in there! It's good in there! Oh yeah!"

"I'm coming, I'm coming, I'm coming. I'm come. I'm come!"

"Aaaawwrrk! So big!"

"Do I like it? Do I like it? Ak. Ak. Shreeee. Do I? Do I? Shreee."

"Okay. Touch my thigh. Higher. Higher. Thigher. There. Here. Here-here. Oop! There-there. Higher—"

And so on. Other parrots seemed for the moment only to be listening, turning their plumed heads this way and that as they considered the odd noises coming over their headphones.

I moved through the office, ignoring the birds as best I could. At the other end of the room there was a white door marked PRIVATE, and under PRIVATE someone had scrawled with a magic marker *third eye third eye set me free*. I tried the handle. The door was unlocked.

It was nothing like the other eyes I'd seen, had none of the grandeur of those several likely bogus and the two or three possibly legitimate contenders for right or left eye, no curved, vaulted retinal space, no darkened chamber, no ritual aspect whatsoever. It was an office with a window, and the window wasn't very large. A modest telescope stood on a tripod at the window, aimed downwards. And it was otherwise an ordinary office: shelves, desk, chair, gray short-hair carpet. There were a few styrofoam cups of cold coffee dregs and a couple of mustard-stained sandwich wrappings on the desk. I went to the window.

From the angle and view I understood that this office was high in the shade of the left ear. If I leaned in close to the window I could see the curve of the left cheek and brow to my right, a slight bulge of neck to my left. My view straight down was partly occluded by the prominent muscle of the left forelimb, which formed a semicircle spanning the width of that downward view—and like a fat man trying to spot his shoetips beneath the swell of his own middle I could just see a nubbin of the left hoof poking out far below that semicircle of muscle. Cheek, brow, neck, shoulder, hoof—that was all I could see of the shape itself, but it was more than enough.

It was what I saw beyond the shape itself that made my mission clear at last, at long last. At long last I understood and recalled as I sat in the chair at the desk and I focused the telescope and took it all in, surveyed the terrain, the field of future battle. Below the limit of the sky ran a perimeter of highway, where passenger cars and commercial trucks full of food and alcohol and durable goods and other treasure whirred ceaselessly past, borne to families in sprawling suburbs blanketed with unimaginable lawns, their lives a throbbing feast of waste and complacency. Distant smokestacks tooted poison into a pale blue sky. In the unseeable distance beyond the highway and the smokestacks men golfed, died, farted, called their secretaries on speakerphones. All lay beyond that boundary where trucks full of ripening avocadoes and bottles of Zinfandel pulsed and rattled to their destinations.

Nearer to the shape was another matter. Everything between that eight-lane horizon line of highway and the hoof of the shape where it met the pavement straight below me was included in a vast gated park, a compound full of gaily painted gingerbread buildings incoherently bedecked with onion domes, doric columns, and porthole windows. Between the buildings zipped little three-wheeled carts with fringed tops, threading lanes amidst

Tilt-a-Whirl rides and coin-speckled fountains and themed restaurants and a small zoo with real walruses, and as well a miniature railroad which was "attacked" as it passed through a grove of trees by "Indians" who were in fact costumed actors. A small Ferris wheel idly circled in space below my window—I could see the tops of the cabs as they reached perihelion, swung, began their descent. I watched and felt my warlike instincts returning. Past the Ferris wheel, paddle boats drifted in a large pond with a plainly fake island, whose cluster of suspiciously fluffy palm trees was brimming with live parrots, not white-plumed parrots like the ones just outside my office in Central Command, but ostentatiously blue and orange parrots with black and orange beaks. To the right, on a granite cliff at a level with the shape's upper chest and neck, sat a mock-medieval castle where pocket dramas were enacted in each window: Rapunzel's hair, Beauty's sleep, Rumpelstiltskin's tantrum. Everywhere families wandered, children gaping, roaring with laughter, vomiting, weeping, dropping ice cream cones, squandering precious resources on cheaply made souvenirs certain to be damaged and abandoned before even reaching the parking lot. These were the children of my enemy, our enemy, yours. A pair of actors costumed as the front and rear of a horse pranced and kicked in tandem, then parted to sign autographs and muss the hair of bewildered children; I understood this actorly horse to be a representation, a celebration of our shape, *this shape*— and I saw postcards and T-shirts too, icons rendered soft and silly for mass consumption. They'd given the shape goggling eyeballs and buck teeth and an endearing scruff of hair in the place of its majestic fearsome eyes and grim-set mouth and noble mane. I saw it and I felt a stir of triumph—we'd lulled them, the morons had actually believed us, they'd wheeled our giant horse into their turf and built this shit factory around it and begun charging admission like it was Graceland, a cute impotent relic, they were so grievously corrupt that they were wearing our grand and mighty instrument of war *on their T-shirts* and they were in the palms of our hands at last. I couldn't hide from myself anymore now, I was awake, awake and sober (though pulling hard on my hip flask, believe me) and full of martial hate and pride and only a little weariness, a trace of regret perhaps—but fuck it, really. Why shouldn't old soldiers get off their lawn chairs and lead pale young men into battle? Did I mean to spend the rest of my days scraping shreds of protein off the grill? Why shouldn't Balkan's bluff get called, why shouldn't Dennis figure out *what really makes his old man tick?* Why shouldn't nearly thirty years of lying in wait, of losing ourselves in distraction and dissolution, of losing sight of our rhyme and reason, our deep-embedded programming, come to a grand and glorious end as we spill out of hiding and smite them high and hard, finally *take it to the hole.* Why shouldn't they get what's coming? I mean, what the fuck was I so afraid of?

The whole shape had been clamoring for my leadership, I saw now—boys had begun to march and salute, to feel the pulse of war without knowing why, and those priestly rumors of *landing* or *returning to the surface* were all part of the same long-slumbering, now-waking impulse to fulfill our destiny. Operatives had told Dennis that he'd have to lead another operative to the third eye—hey, that other operative was me!

I began by strangling and plucking and making a stew out of thirty filthy-mouthed thick-billed parrots. A task considerably rougher on my sloth-softened hands than you might imagine. But those birds weren't bad eating, not bad at all.

Then I started answering the phones.

Interview
with the Crab

THE DOOR TO THE CRAB'S FAUX-GEORGIAN
Tallahassee mansion was opened by a male housekeeper
with a trim red mustache, razor-cut orange hair showing
white at the temples, and the disapproving air of a Mor-
mon or Scientologist functionary. He was dressed, though,
not in Western garb, nor that of a houseboy or cook, but
instead in Chinese robes, so he resembled the token occi-
dental opponent in a martial arts film—the type who lurks
at the side of the primary Asian villain, and is dispatched
by the hero penultimately and with great effort, as a kind
of respectful nod to the western viewer. I wondered if he
might be the same person I'd negotiated with on the tele-

phone, so protractedly, in seeking my interview with his employer. If so, he said nothing to confirm my suspicion, and spoke only deferentially now that I'd been granted access to the house. The foyer and entrance hallway of the crab's home were two stories high, with round-topped cathedral windows that flooded midday illumination on the mute, carpeted surfaces of floor and stairway, on the beige walls and tastefully framed black-and-white photographs, many of which, I noted at a glance, contained images of the crab with grinning visitors to the set of his old television program, *Crab House Days*. The housekeeper closed the door behind me and we stood together dwarfed in pillars of high light and suffocated, it seemed to me, by the Floridian summer heat and the faint odor of proteinous seashore rot that permeated the unconditioned air of the apparently immaculate house.

"He'll see you by the pool, Mr. Lethem."

I wasn't a fan of *Crab House Days* during its original run. The sitcom's five-season heyday as ABC's leading Wednesday night comedy program began during my second year of college, the years when I was least likely to care or even know what was on television or on the covers of supermarket magazines—a condition which actually persisted well into my thirties, when I got cable for the first time, largely in order to keep my eye on my favorite baseball team, the Mets. *Crab House Days* was by then well into its life as a late-night rerun, nobody's idea of hot news. And the crab's brief, unsavory resurgence in the form of the late-night cable reality show *Crab Sex Dorm* was still a few years off then, in the mid-nineties, when I increasingly began to linger, in my channel surfing, over episodes of the now-classic show. I watched *Crab House Days* idly at first, but soon I found myself entranced by the melancholic longueurs which would from time to time open up within the antic behaviors of the giant, house-bound crab and his bawdy, ingenuous human family, the Foorcums.

So many evenings *Crab House Days*, ostensibly a laugh-riot, seemed to end on a wistful note. Pansy Foorcum, the abrasive sexpot daughter who was nonetheless the crab's only reliable confidante, would make herself ready for a date, talking to the crab through the shared wall of their bedrooms as she dressed and applied makeup for a night out, and then go, leaving the crab time and time again to scuttle and fiddle alone in his room. Pansy in many ways played the role of the crustacean's advocate and mediator among the other Foorcums: Sternwood, the crab's loutish father; Grania, the crab's befuddled and mawkish mother; and, of course, the crab's and Pansy's younger sibling, the scene-stealing punk-Libertarian brat Feary Foorcum. Squabbling would cease as all four of the others contemplated Pansy's departure from the house. The other family members seemed saddened, their energies dampened, as though the pleasure in baiting and in-sulting the giant crab were diminished past any value once Pansy was no longer present to stick up for him. For the crab's part, his passive-aggressive ripostes and mordant asides were seemingly lost on their actual targets, Sternwood and Grania and Feary; rather, they were meant for Pansy's ears, and with her departure the crab typically fell to an irate and wounded silence.

Now I allowed myself to be led through the foyer, past a vast, apparently unused dining room, its chairs and table covered with sheets, and through to the back patio. The housekeeper and I stepped through the frame of a sliding glass door. Lawn and gardens extended to high walls of vine-covered brick, fronted with a row of palm trees, and scattered between the house and the limits of the yard were well-tended circular plantings of midget palms and ferns, around an unusually large rectangular pool lipped with a wide margin of peach-colored tile. On the pool's tile, between three slatted wooden deck chairs and a low matching table, squatted the crab, wide and round as a golf cart, yet no higher than my knee.

His armor's sheen wasn't what it had seemed fifteen year's before, on television, or even in the low-resolution video of *Crab Sex Dorm*, a scant three years ago. Perhaps his burnished forest-green and fawn brown color scheme had always been an illusion created by makeup artists. I didn't know and couldn't—wouldn't—ask. Today his mottling was more irregular, his colors black-to-puce, with nothing of the chestnut shine and richness that had always seemed his badge, his pride, no matter how grim the burden of crabdom in a human realm. Otherwise, though, he seemed unchanged. The crab's fragmentary leg, famously amputated in a botched Halloween prank attempted, in a rare instance of filial accord, by Sternwood and Feary, in the show's fourth season, still looked as freshly wounded as ever. The static nature of the crab's injury, and his unwillingness to disguise the rather undelectable gooeyness of the stump, was often given partial credit for the erosion of the show's ratings by the end of that fourth season.

"Will you and Mr. Lethem be needing anything, sir?"

The crab didn't speak, only turned slightly, rattling claws on tile. I'd been warned of his recalcitrance, his hot and cold moods.

"Very good, sir." The housekeeper departed the lawn, leaving me there. No breeze stirred, and apart from my own breathing, and the swim of the sun's pinpoint reflections in the blue of the pool's surface, we might have been captured in the humid noon as in a block of Lucite.

"May I sit?"

Again the crab only scuttled. What the housekeeper had taken as a *no* I took as a *yes*, and found my way to one of the slatted chairs, one facing the crab but not, I hoped, so near as to make him feel intruded upon.

"I don't use a tape recorder, so I hope you don't mind my taking notes."

This drew no response.

"I want you to know, first of all, that I'm a fan. I came to your work quite embarrassingly late, but it's touched me in ways I'm not sure I can describe. But then you've touched so many lives."

The crab now began to issue a sound like a lizard's cry, or perhaps it was the high whine of a distant vacuum cleaner. Without wanting to stare too intently, I searched for signs of a listening attitude in amongst his eye-stalks and feelers.

"I don't mean to suggest I have any special insights that would surprise or enlighten an artist of your stature. Think of me merely as a humble representative of an audience that hasn't forgotten you. If anything, the work grows more resonant over the years."

The sound that signaled the end of the hiss or whine was like a barely detectable yawn. The crab raised one leg, too, as if finger-testing the windless air, or calling a invisible class to order with a single, authoritative gesture— one which also evoked, inevitably, a massive hand flipping the bird to the sky, issuing a fuck-you proclamation to the world at large.

"As the more unimportant local and temporal elements of your show recede into time—I mean, all the dated jokes about long-forgotten current events, and the generic vulgar badinage which is only so typical of network comedy of that era—the singularity of your presence becomes more evident, more timeless and pure. You take part in a continuum of rather desultory figures who stand in symbolic protest against the crassness of the contemporary world, running back through Abe Vigoda and Bob Newhart and Imogene Coca, and pointing all the way, really, to Buster Keaton."

"I've heard that before," said the crab in his loud, gravelly, immensely familiar voice. It startled me almost out of my chair, but I tried to disguise my reaction. "People used to write that all the time, but it's a flat-out lie. I wasn't in-fluenced by Buster Keaton in any way."

"I didn't mean—"

"Nobody has any idea how hard it was for me coming up. It's taken for granted now, kids like you come around, they grew up loving the crab and they figure everybody always loved the crab, the crab must have been some kind of overnight success. Sure, right, but that overnight lasted ten years, no more, no less. Ten years slugging it out on the circuit, little clubs, appearances at lodge dinners and state fairs, riding in the undercarriage of tour buses. I paid my dues a dozen times over and I still feel it right here." The crab reared up, propping on his huge, closed claws, and tapped two legs assertively on his lower shell, as if miming a gut check. "Then you guys come around here talking about Buster Fucking Keaton. Like it was some kind of party for me, this fershlugginer career. 'Hmmm, why, I think I'll just allude to Buster Keaton, that ought to make the eggheads cream their panties.' Tell you the truth, I never saw Buster Keaton when I was coming up because I was too busy busting my chops trying to entertain you people. Never saw Buster Keaton until a couple of years ago and then when I did I didn't see anything I thought was all that great."

"I didn't mean to suggest that your work was in any way derivative—"

"Keaton ever do a show about a crab living in a human family?"

I was silent.

"I'm asking you because I want to know. You seem familiar with Keaton's work, so I'm putting the question to you in great sincerity. Anything with a crab?"

"No."

"Right, that's what I figured. My material is entirely my own. I came to it the same way maybe your precious Keaton or Vigoda came by their own—pure suffering, forged into something of value to others, like crushing a coal into a diamond, at great cost of effort and personal sacrifice, a process you wouldn't know too much about since everything to you is just a big pile of slippery postmodern allusions and references with no soul to speak of, not even any notion that it might be missing one, that there might be something to mourn the loss of—a soul, I mean."

I knew it was not my place to defend myself, here—to point out that it was precisely that essence of existential suffering, or *soul*, if he preferred that term, which had drawn me to his work, made me seek for a description for how such an uncanny and timeless thing had broken out in the vacuous, tinselly environs of network situation comedy. Even as he berated me he was inviting me inside, it appeared to me. My task was to selflessly accept that invitation.

"You say your material is entirely your own. That suffering and sacrifice you speak of lies so close to the surface of your humor. How close were the Foorcums to a portrait of your own family?"

"What are you, like the one guy in the United States with no Google?"

"I'm sorry?"

"I've said a thousand times if I've said it once: I haven't spoken about—or to—my family in over forty years. What makes you think I'm about to sing for you? What was your name, Lehman?"

"Lethem."

"Mr. Lethem, with all respect, go fart on a Wheat Thin. What makes you think today's the day some kid sashays in here and I'm just suddenly in the mood to break my silence for you on a whim, when I wouldn't even sing for that fucker Larry King? Even if I wanted to, my lawyers wouldn't let me. Every single person who ever knew me in that shitheel town has tried to sue me at some point, let alone the members of my beloved goddamn family. Rule one: We speak of the Foorcums as the Foorcums alone, or this is O-V-E-R."

"The Foorcums, then. Are you in touch with Richard Drimpet and Joan Cranewood-Freehan, who played your on-screen parents?"

"These are your questions?" The crab scratched with a single leg against the tile in one direction repeatedly, away from his body, as if trying to strike a match or dislodge something stuck to a foot. His claws, though, lay totally inert, draped before him. "Drimpet and I were off speaking terms by season three, another item you could've peeled off a fan site. Joan used to call me from time to time. She tried to get me to do a guest appearance on that *Snowbirds* show, kept pestering me to come on. But what am I going to say to a bunch of old ladies in a mobile home, you know? 'Follow the sun, chickadees! You haven't got that long to live!'"

"Was it difficult between you and Reg Loud? His embodiment of Feary Foorcum was so memorable, but the two of you were pitted against one another continuously throughout the show. And his behavior after the cancellation was rather bitter." I hoped the crab could follow my leads without having to take offense. Reg Loud had, of course, been jailed for narcotics possession several times after his difficult child-stardom found its nadir in the years following *Crab House Days*. For the crab, I could only assume the ferocity of the character's portrayal of his brother, combined with the young actor's very public woes, resonated deeply with ancient, real-life traumas. I was still circling what seemed to me the main, and perhaps tenderest subject, of Delia Watertree, who'd played Pansy Foorcum.

"Difficult? The opposite. Sometimes in this crazy fucked-up world of show business you meet someone with a real beating heart, someone who matters to you, who knows what it's all worth. Rarer than you might think, unfortunately. Reg is the only thing that kept me going on that show as long as I did."

"I'm surprised to hear you say that. Because his character was usually seen as the crab's tormentor."

"I've taken my licks. That's the business, that's the character. Don't confuse show business for real life, Lethem. Compared to some licks I've taken, that show was all cake and candy and ice cream."

"He flooded your room with sulfur oxide in an attempt to cause you to molt six months early," I said.

"Heh heh. Yeah, that was a good one. One hundred percent the kid's idea, too. Good head on his shoulders. You know, a lot of the best bits came from him and me working together, batting stuff to the writers, free of charge. We'd improv in rehearsals—he was always cutting up, making me pee my pants. Talk about bitter, Loud never got credit for any of that stuff. Head writer walked off with two Emmys. Reg deserved better, much better."

"It's an incredible story. Does he know how you feel about it?" I couldn't recall the last turns in Reg Loud's quite miserable tabloid spiral, except that five or six years earlier he'd resurfaced in a brief stint as a local morning talk show host, spewing right-wing survivalist bilge over the airwaves of some medium-sized Midwestern city, Indianapolis or Cedar Rapids.

"Fuck you trying to imply? Of course he does."

"No offense. I'm glad to hear it."

"None taken."

"I wonder if I could get a chance to talk with him for my story. Do you know how I could get in touch with him?"

The crab fell momentarily silent, but cinched the glistening stump of his amputated leg deep under his lower shell, as if he'd now been involuntarily made to recall some particular hurt.

"He wouldn't care to talk about *Crab House Days*," said the crab. "He's moved on."

"What about Delia Watertree?"

"That bitch."

Delia Watertree, launched to fame as the coarse but irresistible Pansy Foorcum, was the only member of the cast who'd ascended to greater heights since the show's cancellation. The entirety of her subsequent career seemed a kind of long renunciation of the broad and overtly sexual appeal of the Pansy Foorcum character; in her stage and screen roles (she'd never glanced back at television work) she relentlessly played against her natural, peaches-and-cream beauty, favoring roles in glasses or bruise makeup or pants suits or buckskin, playing lawyers, frontier settlers, sexual-assault victims, suicidal writers, vanished aviators, and the like. Nevertheless, a measure of Pansy Foorcum's innocent lustiness thrived almost subliminally within the shell of her prestigious career, confirmed by its apparent absence, as though she and her audience were together rising above prurient thoughts in rewarding her with Oscar and Tony nominations for her nobler roles. Too, her quiet, reflective mannerisms still recalled the poignancy she'd evoked in spells of gentleness toward her sitcom sibling, the housebound crab.

"She was lovely to your character," I said, speaking softly now. "A viewer would have thought you and Pansy were full of feeling for one another. You often seemed united against the others—Feary, and your parents. As if you two alone shared a sense of dreamy possibility about what might lay outside the space of the house—beyond the circumscribed sensibility of the Foorcum family."

"You go on telling yourself what you want to hear," said the crab. "Meanwhile I'll bet you watched her like the rest of America's teenage boys, with one hand in your pants and your tongue pressed to the screen."

I chose not to point out the impossibility of the physical arrangement he proposed. It occurred to me that it might, in fact, be possible to watch a television screen while lapping at it with one's antennae. "I remember when you asked her not to go to the prom, since you couldn't go—"

"Listen. You want the skinny on Delia? That little floozy used to cavort around the set with no underwear on, just to drive me crazy, knowing nobody else could see, knowing I'd never say anything. Believe me, the carpet did *not* match the drapes. She'd put her foot up on a chair and start re-lacing her high-tops, right in my face, trying to get me to flub lines."

"That's astonishing."

"Believe it. You know what else? At night, after the whole rest of the cast and crew had gone, she'd bring guys back and do them, sometimes two at a time, real marathon stuff, right in the next room, so I couldn't get a minute of sleep. What a mouth on her, too, always crying out 'make me your little whore' and telling these guys it was the biggest thing she'd ever seen, how she was so frightened it would hurt her—"

Now I was certain the crab was confused. "But, you didn't *really* live in that room—" I began. I wondered whether in fact his memory had slipped back to an earlier time, to that other family of which he'd sworn he'd never speak. Perhaps Pansy Foorcum had merged in his mind with an unnamed sister in another house, long ago. The difficulty, of course, was that it was equally likely that in his confusion he'd conflated *Crab House Days* with *Crab Sex Dorm*. That short-lived reality show had been notoriously lavish in its use of crab-point-of-view camera placements.

The creature appeared not to hear me. He carried on muttering about Pansy's sexual theatrics, reproducing what he'd supposedly overheard through the wall, playing both voices aloud as if performing a *Punch and Judy* show—a private litany aired, it seemed to me, for reasons having nothing to do with our interview. At last he reached a pitch and then quit abruptly, his words replaced with the high whining sound he'd treated me to earlier, and then with the distinct yawn. "Keep that in mind next time you see her begging for money for African famine relief," he concluded. "She's probably got nothing on under her Florence Nightingale costume, either. That dame gets her jollies from pity."

I opted to chalk the crab's freewheeling animus up to show-business envy, at the prestige accorded to the sole performer who'd shaken the career curse of the franchise. "What's in the cards for you?" I asked, not wishing to hear more. "Is this a firm retirement? Do you long to reconnect with your audience?"

"I get calls every day, believe you me." The crab stirred a claw, his minor rather than major, which still lay unmoving. He ratcheted the smaller pinchers wide and turned them toward his face, as if miming a telephone receiver.

"I'm sure you do."

"I'm telling you, some of the pitches I've heard. Crazy stuff. Hoo-wee. I had some rappers out here the other day. Everything nowadays is gangsta, gangsta, gangsta. Those guys are revitalizing show business, if you ask me. But I don't really see a place for myself in the mix."

"So, you'll rest on your laurels," I suggested.

"What fucking laurels? You see one goddamn laurel around here? If you do, it probably blew over from the next yard. Hah. Sorry, I just hate that word—*laurels.*"

"I only wondered if you're content not to practice your art."

"Listen, I'm keeping busy." The crab withdrew and shuttered his claw now, seeming to grow reflective.

"I didn't mean anything—"

"I know you didn't, kid."

"You've got nothing to prove to anyone," I said softly.

"Don't patronize me."

I fell to silence. The crab shifted, sighed, rattled. The day had turned, too, clouds deflecting the high bleaching sun, and announcing themselves as gray mountains in the oscillating mirror of the pool.

"Look, Lehman. You want a scoop? I'm hatching a major comeback. You can be the first. I'm saying major major. You understand? When this thing blows, there'll be no keeping a lid on it, I promise you."

"A premise for a show?"

"Big show, of sorts."

"Please."

"Follow me. I'd tell you to *walk this way*, only you've heard that one before."

Startlingly, the crab was on the go. He moved awfully fast for a being that had seemed wrought in rusted ironwork a moment before. Clicking his way off the tile-work, he slid across the grass, past me, and toward the left side of the house. The lawn dipped to a basement door there, portal to a half-submerged, windowless lower level with the appearance of a garage or workshop, perhaps. I stood, stuffed my pad and ballpoint into my pants pocket, and hurried to join him.

"Go ahead, open the door," he said.

I tried the handle, which turned easily, and pushed the door inside. The darkness was enough that from the brightness of the day I couldn't make anything out, within. I stepped back, uncertain.

Crab House Days had, of course, made much of the conceit that its title character was trapped in his bedroom, yet I recalled from some footage from *Crab Sex Dorm* how he could transverse human doorways by tipping himself dexterously on one side. The crab did this now, gripping the doorframe neatly with his claws and virtually rolling himself through the doorway. Inside, he dropped back to the unpainted cement floor. I followed, leaving the door open behind me. The basement was cool and conveyed an intense marine smell, like that of an aquarium. Low fluorescent fixtures shone a dim green light, from what ap-

peared to be special bulbs, perhaps like those for illumi-
nating plants or animals in a zoo display of creatures unused to direct sunlight. As my eyes accustomed themselves
to the dark I saw that we were surrounded by dozens of
immense water tanks, the murk and silt within them glowing in the greenish light.

Another figure stepped from the rear, startling me. It
was Feary Foorcum—or rather, Reg Loud. Loud was
cloaked in a white lab coat, and still wore his hair in his
signature ragged punk cut. He was also still of a childish
stature, though he'd grown stocky, and his once brattish
features were withered and creased with deep lines of cyn-
icism and age—he seemed still too young to be an adult,
and far too old to be in his early forties, as a quick calcu-
lation suggested he ought to be. But then perhaps he had
been playing younger than his real age on *Crab House
Days*, like so many child stars have done.

"Reg, this is Mr. Lehman. He's come to have a look at
my quote-unquote comeback."

Reg Loud stuck out a horny, trollish hand. "Pleased to
meet you," he said in the terribly familiar voice, a sort of
parroty squawk, with which he'd hectored both his parents and crab for all five seasons, filling their ears with his
crank Libertarian views. "You're one of the first to see the
babies."

"Babies?"

"Have a look."

I squinted in close to the nearest of the tanks. I spotted
them now, realized in fact that they'd been visible all along

but that I'd mistaken them for sworls of colored shadow in the glow. Behind the glass swam hundreds upon hundreds of tiny, translucent green-yellow crabs. Each was perhaps three-quarters of an inch wide. They coursed over one another in a giddy chaos of youthful agitation, like puppies, or sperm.

I moved to the next tank and found more. I was no savant, but a rough guess suggested there might be tens of thousands of the tiny crabs in the damp, humming basement with us there, a slushy riot of life, a throbbing army of creatures.

"Maybe you can help me decide what to call it," said the crab. "I keep vacillating between *Revenge of the Crab* and *Crab World Domination.*"

"I like *Crab World Domination*," I said. "It suggests more continuity with your earlier work."

"That's a point," said the crab.

"They're all him, you understand," said Reg Loud.

"Sorry?"

"All him," Loud repeated. "They're clones."

"I see. How soon will they be, uh, ready?"

"They won't attain his mature size for twenty years," said Reg Loud. "But they'll be ready for release in three or four."

"Not so much of a comedy this time," I mused.

"You could say that," consented the crab.

"Perhaps more of a disaster movie, or a cable miniseries?"

"Do you know anything about global warming, Mr. Lehman?" said Reg Loud.

"Of course."

"You say you do, yet do you understand that the ten warmest years in recorded history have occurred since 1983? *Seven* of them since 1990. Some of us will be better adapted to the coming changes than others."

"In other words," said the crab, "this really has nothing at all to do with television."

"The *evolution* will not be televised," chortled Loud. "The mocked *shell* inherit the earth."

"Don't worry, Lehman, we'll still need historians of television comedy, or rather we'll need them again in a few dozen centuries, when crabs develop television. Your work won't be in vain."

"Are they all comedians like their father?" I asked.

"We'll see, won't we?"

"Yes, I suppose so."

"Let's leave them now. Thank you, Reg."

I took one last glance back at those rows of tanks that glowed, it seemed to me now, much as if lit by cathode ray. I wondered if the radiant, morsel-sized clones, who so resembled cartoons or plastic toys, would truly be fit to outlive us, to occupy some brave new world. It was hardly anything I'd mention to the crab, but I had an intuition his progeny might share his tropism for the human world, and be bereft without us. Perhaps this was my naïve projection, an inability to fathom a universe without myself in it. But the crab himself had never known the sea, so far as I understood. He'd been born and raised in a landlocked state, in custody of a solidly middle-class, if not exactly loving, family.

"Close the door," the crab commanded. He scrabbled up the hump of grass, and back to his tile shelf. I wondered whether he ever even so much as dipped himself in the pool. It looked unsullied by any of the secretions I now detected in both dried and fresh traces on the tile and lawn. I followed back to the poolside, but didn't retake my chair. I think we both sensed the interview was nearly at an end.

"You get what you came for, Lehman?"

"Far more, I'd have to say."

"Well, I've got one question for you."

"Certainly."

He paused, perhaps sinking into himself again for a moment. I couldn't keep from thinking that the sight of the blank greenish tide of successors had made him every bit as melancholy as it had me. Before he spoke again he made another of his strange wheezy yawning sounds, and trickled his legs, including the amputated stump, along the tiles, quite softly. Each of his claws stirred, too, though they didn't open.

"I really caused you to think of Keaton or Newhart? Because I just don't see it."

I was astonished it still mattered to him. "It was a stray thought, only intended as a compliment."

"Those figures are much milder than my character, at least after the first season. I always felt I was more in the line of a classic slow-burn specialist, someone like Edgar Kennedy or William Frawley or Beatrice Arthur."

"There's validity in those comparisons," I admitted. The fact that the crustacean could even supply these names made nonsense of his earlier claims not to have known Keaton's films, and of his stiff refusal to consider tracing the lineage of influence behind his own work. But I was hardly keen to confront his inconsistencies.

"Listen, nobody but you and me even remembers those names," he said, hardening again, as if he'd allowed an instant of vanity to bare his defenses. "You need to get yourself a life that's free of this kind of academic horseshit. If I can move forward without wallowing, it's the least you can do."

Had he eschewed wallowing? It was another claim I didn't care to refute. "I'm grateful for the advice."

"Mr. Boniface can call you a cab."

"That's fine. I'll wait in front."

"Lehman?"

"Yes?"

"One thing I ask. I don't want you to lie about me, you understand? I don't care what anyone thinks. Every word, every belch and fart, is on the goddamn record. You got this? Tell the truth about me."

I promised the crab I would try.

ALSO BY JONATHAN LETHEM

AS SHE CLIMBED ACROSS THE TABLE

Alice has left her boyfriend, Philip, for nothing. A particle physicist, she and her colleagues have created a void that they have taken to calling Lack. But Lack is a nullity with taste. To Alice this translates as an irresistible personality. To Philip, it makes Lack an unbeatable rival, for how can he win Alice back from something that has no flaws—because it has no qualities.

Fiction/0-375-70012-9

THE FORTRESS OF SOLITUDE

The Fortress of Solitude is the story of Dylan Ebdus growing up white and motherless in downtown Brooklyn in the 1970s. Dylan has one friend, a black teenager, also motherless, named Mingus Rude. As Lethem follows their friendship, he creates a rich and emotionally gripping canvas of race and class, superheroes, gentrification, funk, hip-hop, graffiti-tagging, loyalty, and memory.

Fiction/0-375-72488-5

GIRL IN LANDSCAPE

In this deliriously original book, thirteen-year-old Pella Marsh emigrates with her family to the Planet of the Archbuilders. These enigmatic aborigines baffle and frighten their human visitors. As the spikily independent Pella becomes an uneasy envoy between two species, *Girl in Landscape* deftly interweaves themes of exploration and otherness, loss and sexual awakening.

Fiction/0-375-70391-8

MOTHERLESS BROOKLYN

Lionel Essrog, an orphan whose Tourettic impulses drive him to rip apart our language in startlingly original ways, works for small-time mobster Frank Minna. When Frank is fatally stabbed, Lionel's world is suddenly topsy-turvy, and this outcast who has trouble even conversing attempts to untangle the threads of the case while trying to keep the words straight in his head.

Fiction/0-375-72483-4

VINTAGE CONTEMPORARIES
Available at your local bookstore, or call toll-free to order:
1-800-793-2665 (credit cards only).